KU-072-815

Revenge Burns Deep

Tough army scout Green River Jim Claymaker is heading east on a mission of the heart. But his plans are upset when, passing through the Costilla Valley, a devastating prairie fire, started deliberately by an adversary, claims the life of an old friend who perishes in the blaze while scouting for a wagon train.

Ira Gemmel, a cunning Indian trader, has his own devious reasons for preventing the wagon train from reaching Santa Rosa, New Mexico. The son of a Comanche chief is shot and Gemmel blames Claymaker and the settlers. Claymaker's proficiency and courage are tested to the limit to bring the real perpetrator to justice and save the pioneers from the wrath of the avenging Indians.

Revenge Burns Deep

Ethan Flagg

A Black Horse Western

ROBERT HALE · LONDON

© Ethan Flagg 2016
First published in Great Britain 2016

ISBN 978-0-7198-1805-9

Robert Hale Limited
Clerkenwell House
Clerkenwell Green
London EC1R 0HT

www.halebooks.com

Typeset by
Derek Doyle & Associates, Shaw Heath
Printed and bound in Great Britain by
CPI Antony Rowe, Chippenham and Eastbourne

ONE

DECISION OF THE HEART

The lone rider nudged his horse up the shallow grade.

At its crest, he paused to light a cigarillo. He was a tall man on the wrong side of forty. The broad-brimmed plainsman hat was pulled down low over deep-set eyes to shade out the harsh sunlight. Numerous furrows gave the weather-beaten face a ruggedly handsome aspect now fixed in an unusually solemn mood.

His thoughts were occupied by the purpose of his journey. That said, the rider still retained the capacity to absorb every facet of the barren landscape that stretched away towards the eastern horizon. Being an army scout, his life depended on his ability to read sign and sniff out danger.

His duties scouting for the army were tough and gruelling, Jim Claymaker would not have wished it any other way. An enviable reputation had made him famous throughout the western territories for his tracking prowess in curbing the growing threat from rebellious Indian resistance.

He sympathized with the tribal claims that their lands were being taken over by the ever-increasing numbers of white immigrants. The need for new territory to accommodate the settlers was indeed becoming remorseless.

But the scout's responsibilities were to his own kind. Raiding parties that killed and tortured innocent travellers needed to be restrained. Claymaker was the man the army relied upon to uphold and maintain authority in a volatile period of American expansion. It was a relentlessly demanding task. And he was not getting any younger.

He sucked hard on the thin tube of tobacco allowing its effect to concentrate his thoughts. For Green River Jim was at a turning point in his life.

Numerous hints had been dropped to Colonel Sourby, the commander of Fort Benson, that the time for him to step down was fast approaching. Perhaps he would head for California to grow oranges, his favourite fruit, and maybe raise a few kids as well. But for that he needed to find a wife with whom he could settle down.

The days of leading patrols through Indian territory and negotiating treaties with the tribes had taken their toll. Long thick hair, once black as the ace of spades, was now streaked with too many silvery threads. His lean frame was scared and pitted by innumerable encounters with hostile redskins, not to mention grizzly bears.

There were also the run-ins with unscrupulous traders who tried to fleece the gullible tribes. And others who had sold bad meat to the army. The latest conflict had been with a devious rat based in the town of Santa Rosa, New Mexico. Ira Gemmel ran the only general store in the town. By fair means or foul, mainly the latter, dubious deals had made certain that his was the sole surviving establishment.

At the moment, however, Green River Jim had other things on his mind.

The renowned army scout had acquired his moniker from fur trapping up in the mountain fastness of south west Wyoming. But the heyday of the mountain men had passed and with it the need for beaver pelts. Silk had taken over in the making of gentlemen's hats. Claymaker's intimate knowledge of the terrain and its native inhabitants had made him an ideal recruit for the army when the tribes had rebelled against invasion of their lands.

The scout shook his proud shock of hair at the recollection of his latest fracas. 'This kinda life is becoming a mite too hectic for a guy of my age,' he muttered aloud to his faithful appaloosa stallion. 'Don't you reckon, old fella?'

To a frontiersman who lived most of his days alone, the horse was his only constant companion. It was inevitable, therefore, that he addressed the animal as an equal. Blaize nodded his noble head as if in communion with his master's dilemma.

'But have I made the right decision? That's the question I keep asking myself.' Again he sucked hard on the cigarillo allowing the blue smoke to twine from the corner of his mouth. It was a query that only Green River Jim could answer.

A meadow lark, perched close by on a rock, chirruped as if querying the unspoken doubt now assailing the scout's thoughts. In truth, he had been wondering about the momentous undertaking upon which he was now engaged since filling out the application form some weeks before. Was he being foolishly naïve?

For Jim Claymaker had done the unthinkable. At least according to his associates whose opinions he had sought, though only on a tentative basis. Most had spurned the idea. It was not for the likes of them.

The rugged army scout had chosen a mail-order bride.

Guys in his line of work rarely came in contact with suitable marriage partners. In the west that he inhabited, such dames were a rare breed. Days stuck out in the wilds could get mighty lonesome, especially the nights when a man dreamed of a warm body to tingle his loins.

Women of dubious morals were easy enough to find. Cat Houses abounded in every settlement catering to the basic needs of frontiersmen. But they were not the sort with whom a man would choose to settle down. For every eligible female there had to be at least ten guys seeking her affections. Poor odds for anybody in the marriage stakes. Especially for one who spent much of his time in the wilderness.

It had all come about two months before.

A much-thumbed catalogue advertising suitable ladies wishing to meet up with partners had been discarded by an old buddy. The two pals had arrived in the New Mexico town of Cimarron in search of some much needed rest and relaxation.

Coyote Ross Calhoun had poured scorn on the notion. 'A guy who can't spark his own gal has to be plum desperate to go for these dames,' he averred flinging the catalogue aside. A derisive scowl indicated his disdain for the contents. And that included those who might choose to sneak down the mail order trail.

Claymaker hadn't given it much thought at the time, merely nodding in agreement. The two men were sitting in the barber's shop awaiting much-needed treatment following months in the mountain wilderness of southern Colorado.

They had been hunting down a band of headstrong Comanche bucks who had become angered by settlers trespassing on their lands. Tracking them had been a long and dangerous undertaking. The hostiles had attacked numerous isolated farmsteads killing the occupants. But in the end, Broken Lance had been worn down by the dogged determination of his pursuers.

Army scouts respected the native inhabitants of the high plains. Many had adopted their dress code and some had even taken Indian wives. But the murder of innocent settlers had to be avenged in no uncertain terms.

The final confrontation at Coal Creek had been brutal and decisive. Against Claymaker and his body of Indian hunters armed with the latest repeating rifles, Broken Lance's forlorn band had stood no chance. Many had been killed, others captured. Unfortunately for the pursuers, Broken Lance himself had managed to escape back into the mountains and still posed a threat.

On their arrival in Cimarron, the barber's shop was their first port of call. The two men were given a wide berth by others who had called in. Excuses accompanied the wrinkled snouts as customers indicated they would return later. The odious reek from the tattered buckskins worn by the two scouts was impossible to ignore.

Even the resilient barber, used to all manner of clients, had been forced to spray their garments with scented water before allowing them to remain on the premises. A hot bath outside in the back yard had at least made them presentable for the final attentions offered by Razorback Jones.

Calhoun was first in the chair. Awaiting his turn, Claymaker's gaze shifted towards the much despised catalogue. He was of a similar mind to his pal. But nonetheless the scout was still intrigued by the contents.

Having been scalped, preened and pomaded, Coyote Ross emitted a deep sigh of enjoyment. 'Gee, that was good,' he announced admiring his much-altered appearance in the mirror. 'Who is that handsome dude?'

'Can't see anyone matching that description in here,' returned Claymaker scratching his thick pate of greasy hair. 'Just some old has-been kidding himself. But I soon will.' He stood up ready to take his own place in the barber's chair.

'Not a chance, old buddy,' replied Calhoun accepting the joshing in good part. 'Madam Seagrove's top gals are gonna be swooning over me when I saunter in there. You can have the rest with my blessing.' The two pals chuckled at their good-natured bantering. 'But what's needed first are a few jugs of cold beer over at the Blue Bottle saloon to get me in the right mood.'

'I'll see you over there when Razorback has turned me into a real strutting dandy,' declared Claymaker waving aside his buddy's disdainful bout of guffawing.

It was only later that night in his room at the National Hotel that the chief scout studied the contents of the berated catalogue in more detail. It was certainly an eye-opening parade of gentile female clients wishing to communicate with possible bachelors. The clear aim was to establish a rapport for the purpose of marriage.

An eastern lady called Eliza Farnham was the first person to recognize the need for a service that introduced the sexes to each other in a responsible and organized manner. That was back in 1849 following the exit of thousands of eligible young men heading

11

for the California goldfields.

Her initial foray into this new venture was adver-
tised in a San Francisco newspaper. It immediately
caught hold of the popular imagination. Thousands
of lonely diggers were eager for female company. But
only three girls arrived on that first ship causing much
aggravation. The system eventually settled down and
became a thriving means of drawing like partners
together.

By the 1870s, the catalogues had become much
more sophisticated and informative. The advertise-
ments had also become rather dubious in their
alluring descriptions. A great deal of chicanery and
duplicity was employed by women eager to enhance
their prospects. False bosoms, heavily applied face
paint, padding and wigs frequently gave them a far
more enticing appearance than nature had intended.

With money paid up front, the gullible punters
were often sadly disillusioned when their paramours
finally arrived.

Jim Claymaker was well aware of this trickery. He
was adamant that such deception would not fool him.
The various letters in the catalogue from satisfied
clients assured him that good marriages arranged in
this unusual manner abounded.

Without mentioning a word to anybody, especially
Coyote Ross, the scout began writing to one particular lady who had taken his fancy. Over the coming
months, various missives passed back and forth.
Eventually Claymaker suggested that they meet for
the first time at the railroad junction of Walsenburg

in Colorado.

He had waited in vain for a reply. Had the woman got cold feet and backed out? The greenhorn wife-seeker was in a quandary. What should he do?

The proposed liaison was in ten day's time. So he had decided to head for the junction, hoping and praying that she would arrive.

Again he pulled hard on the cigarillo. It helped to calm his jangling nerves. The nearer he came to the momentous endeavour, the more panicky he became. Facing down Broken Lance and his deadly bunch had been child's play compared to this. Each time he stopped, his hand itched to swing the stallion around and head back to the mountains where he felt safe.

Then, the face of Lavinia Stapleton swam into view. She sure was a peach. He dug into the pocket of his buckskin jacket and fished out the crumpled picture. And for the umpteenth time, read her latest missive. Even the delicate sweep of her hand sent a shiver rolling down his spine. A sigh of contentment issued from between clenched teeth. It was instantly replaced by a lowered frown. Once again, doubt gnawed at his vitals. Had he done the right thing? And was she still of the same mind?

Only a face-to-face liaison would answer that question. All he could hope for now was that she would arrive on the westbound train at the time he had proposed.

Nudging Blaize forward, he was about to continue his journey when something caught his watchful eye.

TWO

FLAMING AUGUST

Flocks of birds were heading across his path. Nothing unusual there, but for the fact that they appeared to be in panic-stricken flight. Squealing and cawing like demented sirens. And not only birds. Coyotes, deer and jack rabbits were heading in the same direction.

Something had clearly scarred them witless.

'What's happening over there, Blaize?' Claymaker's puzzlement was echoed by the appaloosa which sensed the terror born on the gusting plains wind. 'Guess we ought to investigate,' declared the scout spurring down the shallow grade and up on to the far ridgeback. Cresting the apex, the full horror of the alarming animal stampede was revealed in all its terrifying furore.

'Thunderation! It's a darned fire!'

The horrifying outbreak that all plainsmen feared was sweeping down the valley of Costilla Creek. And the rampant inferno was chasing a stampeding herd of buffalo in its wake. Claymaker quickly concluded that with the wind blowing from the west it would keep moving, unchallenged, devouring the long grass and everything else in its headlong path.

Fire hazards were most prevalent in the hot season. And August was the deadliest of months. They could happen for any number of reasons. A discarded cigarette butt, a piece of glass reflecting the sun's harsh rays. Even flashes of lightning could set them off. In the earlier days of the frontier, Indian tribes had deliberately caused controlled outbreaks to improve pasture. But since the arrival of the hated white eyes, fires were now regarded as a threat to life and property.

The only way to stop them was by establishing firebreaks with controlled blazes. But this was dangerous and any misjudgement could easily go awry. If cattle were in the vicinity cowboys would slaughter and skin a beast and drag it across the front of the flames, frequently changing direction to prevent injury to the horses' hoofs. Apart from that, the only thing to do was pray for rain.

A sky of deepest azure held no hope in that latter respect. All that could stop the rampant inferno was a broad span of water. Certainly not Costilla Creek which was little more than a trickle. The nearest river of any size was the Canadian to the east.

Claymaker's keen gaze picked out an alien presence in the centre of the charging herd. Quickly extracting his telescope, he focussed in. A sharp intake of breath followed. It was a mounted rider.

'If'n I ain't mistaken, that's Coyote Ross down there.' The alarmed cry elicited a whiney from Blaize. 'And he's in big trouble. That horse he's riding looks like it's thrown a shoe.'

What his old buddy was doing in this neck of the woods did not impinge on the army scout's thoughts. They had not been in contact for a couple of months. All that mattered now was saving his friend from certain death. One slight error in the fleeing horse's stride and Calhoun would be a goner. Once started, nothing would stop a rampaging herd of heavy-weights.

Claymaker urged his horse to the gallop. Firing his pistol into the air, he managed to force the rampaging brutes to one side allowing him to break through the bunching pack. Calhoun's centralized position was not a good place to be. The scout yelled and hollered, waving his hat and firing until the gun clicked on empty while giving Blaize his head.

The air was thick with yellow dust. A thundering howl akin to the bellowing of a thousand hounds from hell hammered at his ears. Could anybody survive within such a chaotic melee? Especially on a lame cayuse. A blurred outline resolved itself through the thick soup. Claymaker gritted his teeth. Determination to rescue his friend was written in stark lines across his weathered features.

But ill-luck had befallen the trapped scout. A panicking bull veered to one side crashing into Calhoun's mount. Already at a disadvantage, the beleaguered animal stumbled, tossing its rider high into the air. A choking yelp of fear issued from the stricken victim's dry throat. It was snatched away amid the ear-blasting cacophony. One second he was there, the next gone.

How could any human being survive such a tumble?

As luck would have it, the bulk of the stampede had passed enabling Claymaker to scatter the tail-enders.

Once the buffalo had passed on, the dust quickly dispersed leaving an untidy hump of human flotsam splayed out across a ravaged stand of sagebrush. Of Calhoun's horse there was no sign. Neither was there any discernible movement from the fallen rider. A lump stuck in Claymaker's throat as he dashed across to tend his stricken comrade.

But the danger was not past.

Already, clutching tongues of flame were licking at the still form.

'We gotta save him, Blaize. Go boy!' The croaking holler was laced with panic as Claymaker urged the stallion towards its namesake. Nothing was like to frighten an animal more than a fire gone berserk. But Blaize held his nerve. The horse appeared to understand the desperation in his master's fearful cry. It charged across the flat bottomland unheeding of the imminent peril.

The dense pall of black smoke spewing from the roaring conflagration was as much a threat as the grasping flames to the survival of Coyote Ross. His buddy ignored the burning heat that was already singeing his own buckskin jacket. There was no time to lose. He grabbed up the stricken man and threw him across the saddle. A stifled groan issued from Calhoun's throat.

At least he was still alive.

'Steady, boy, easy does it,' he gentled the big stallion ruffling his twitching ears. 'Don't you go getting the jitters. We're almost out of this.' Then he slapped the horse on the rump urging Blaize over to the welcoming waters of Costilla Creek. Following at a run, he splashed across the shallows to the far side.

'Leave me, Jim,' the injured man gasped out. 'Save yourself. I'm all stove in.' His breathing was laboured and shallow. 'Them buffalo don't give a tinker's cuss who or what they trample underhoof.'

The rescuer was not listening. He was well aware that their current position could only be a temporary refuge. Already the stretching tendrils of flame had leapt across the narrow reach. 'Easy there, old buddy,' he chided. 'Don't try to talk. Ain't no way I'm leaving you in this hell hole.'

Claymaker doused his friend's body with water as the rampant flames consolidated their hold on the tinder dry grass and scrub. But this was no time for dithering.

'We gotta get you out of here, Ross,' Claymaker averred carefully lifting the injured man once again into the saddle. 'Brogden's Reach is the nearest trading post. You can rest up there while I head for the sawbones at Trinidad.'

Much as he tried taking it easy, the constant jolting was agony for the broken body. Coyote Ross stood the pain for as long as possible. But soon he was pleading with his benefactor to set him down. 'I can't take anymore, Jim. It's too much. Just set me down so's I can die in peace.'

Claymaker was loath to abandon his partner. But the guy's beseeching wails clutched at his heart-strings. He pulled to a halt and gently laid the poor guy on the hard ground. 'We'll stay here for spell,' he said trying to make the shattered frame more com-fortable. 'Then I'll go on alone and bring back help. . . .'

'No time for that,' the injured man croaked. His breath came in short wheezing gasps. It sounded to Claymaker like he had a punctured lung. But Calhoun somehow managed to rally. Forcing himself on to one elbow, he gripped his friend's arm. 'I'm through here . . . this is trail's end for Coyote Ross. . . .' His eyes closed, the leathery features sagging.

Claymaker knew that his old pal's time had come. The final curtain was falling on a life cut short. A tear etched a path down the tough scout's cheek. He roughly brushed it aside.

Then once again, Calhoun perked up. His eyes flickered open.

'Guess you're wondering what old Coyote is doing out here . . . I'm the scout for a wagon train bound for Santa Rosa. We've come from Concordia in Kansas and have been on the trail for five weeks.'

He paused to draw breath. It was an ugly rasping sound. Claymaker knew his old friend was teetering on the brink. But he made to assure Coyote that everything would be fine. 'Rest easy, buddy, I can't have you pegging out on. . . .'

But the injured man interjected before he could finish. 'You need to save them folks, Jim. They're heading right into the teeth of that fire. If'n they enter the Costilla Valley, there'll be no room to swing about. . . .' Calhoun's plea had exhausted him. He desperately sucked in ever shallower gulps of air. 'Leave me here and get to riding, or the whole caboodle will be engulfed. . . . A fire this size will wipe out every living soul.'

A strangled gurgle rumbled in his throat. The shattered body convulsed as his heart finally gave out. Then he sank back, head lolling to one side.

Coyote Ross Calhoun had made his final scouting trip, and it had cost him dear. Claymaker was utterly distraught. His head drooped. Right to the very end, the tough jasper's only thought had been for the safety of those in his care.

'You sure lived up to the code of the frontier and no mistake, old friend,' he averred. 'Nobody could have asked any more of you.'

But if what the guy had said held water, there was no time to dally. That wagon train was heading for a run-in with nature flexing her muscles in the most virulent manner. The scout quickly covered the body with rocks. It was only a makeshift grave, but would have to suffice.

'That'll keep the predators from violating you until I can arrange a proper burial,' he assured the late

departed soul. Removing his hat, Jim Claymaker
starred down at the pile of stones. His eyes misted
over with regret. 'You can rest easy now, old pal. I'd
sure like to have said some words from the good
book. Guess that'll have to wait a spell. Those folks
need to be warned. *Adios, compadre!*'

Minutes later, Blaize was galloping along the crest
of the ridge bordering Costilla Creek. The wind had
picked up and was sweeping the rampant conflagration down the narrow valley destroying everything in
its wake. The scout could only pray that the train had
not yet reached the entrance to the valley.

Still grieving over the loss of a much admired old
comrade, Green River Jim Claymaker rode with a
heavy heart. An hour later he emerged from the con-
fines of the valley. And he was only just in time.

The wagon train was heading straight for the
entrance to the Costilla that Ross Calhoun had been
scouting. Another ten minutes and they would have
been trapped in there. The notion sent a shiver down
Claymaker's back. If it hadn't been for the dead scout,
disaster would have been the inevitable consequence.

The wagon train was a small affair by normal stan-
dards. No more than twenty-five wagons each with a
team of four horses. Known as Prairie Schooners they
were an enduring symbol of enterprise in the old
west. The billowing white canvas covers made them
look like a fleet of ships floating across the waves of
grass.

He assumed this one had been following the Santa
Fe Trail. It must have branched off the regular route

to follow a new spur called the Cimarron Cut-Off. This recent discovery was meant to save time.

The new section avoided the longer and rougher mountainous route via Benson Fort and the Raton Pass. Although flatter and shorter than the main trail, the Cut-Off posed its own hazards. Alkali dust storms across the waterless Cimarron desert made for a precarious crossing. On the other hand, spring floods could turn the sandy wasteland into an ocean of clinging mud.

Although Claymaker had never previously ridden this way, Coyote must have reckoned the Cut-Off to be a good alternative. On this occasion it had unfortunately proved fatal to the intrepid scout. Claymaker promised himself that his friend's untimely death would not be in vain.

He waved his hat in the air to attract the attention of the man leading the line of wagons. Even at that distance he instantly recognized the distinctive figure of Griff Reed. A retired mountain man known throughout the territories as Pop, he was a stubborn old cuss who refused to acknowledge that times had moved on.

Like many others of his kind who trapped the mountain streams, Jim Claymaker included, Pop had been forced to seek employment elsewhere when the pickings declined and trends changed. Rather than adopting the standard broad brimmed hat now favoured by many frontiersmen, he had stuck with the traditional coonskin cap.

And none of these new-fangled repeaters for Pop

Reed. The aging yet reliable Hawken long rifle resting across his legs was like a third arm.

Nevertheless, he was a good solid man to lead naïve settlers across the unknown terrain. Without intrepid pioneers like him to guide them, the settlers would never make the promised land of their dreams. Claymaker smiled as the old guy stroked his thick grey beard clearly tossing over what his rheumy eyes had spotted.

'Hold up there, Pop,' he called out.

'Is that you Green River?' the rasping voice scarred by too much hard liquor exclaimed in surprise. 'Ain't seen you in a coon's age. What you so all fired up about? Some Comanche buck found you spooning with his squaw?' A hearty guffaw readily approved the old timer's own snappy crack. All the same, he held up an arm signalling the lead wagon to haul rein.

But Claymaker was not smiling. 'It ain't me that's fired up, Pop,' he retorted pointing to his rear. 'There's a blaze ramping down the Costilla and its heading right this way.'

He went on to quickly relate the grim tidings of Ross Calhoun's sad demise.

Reed's eyes bulged. 'Gee that's bad news about Coyote. All the folks here thought the world of him. We owe the guy a lot. Best scout I've had with me since I started leading these trains back in '68. So that's why all them buffalo were in such an almighty hurry.'

'You owe him your lives too. Best way to prove he didn't die in vain is to pull off the trail and head for

23

the Canadian River.' An anxious glance towards the Costilla Valley saw his back stiffening. Smoke was already drifting above the ridgeline. 'Keep on this route and it'll trap you for sure.'

'The nearest crossing point is five miles north of here at Sublette Narrows,' the wagon master declared, 'but it'll take time to turn the wagons.'

'There ain't no time to lose then, Pop.'

Swinging around, Griff Reed galloped off down the line of Conestoga wagons instructing each driver to make the turn and get into a new formation. By the time the twenty-five wagons were ready to head off on the new course, the fire had broken free of the narrow Costilla and was avidly devouring the prairie grass beyond.

With no hindrance to its rampant advance and a strengthening wind, it would be touch and go whether the cumbersome wagons could escape the clutching tentacles of flame. A life-and-death struggle now followed to safely reach the vital river crossing point in time.

What Green River Jim and Pop Reed didn't realize was that the fire had been started deliberately. And the perpetrators were watching their every movement from a cluster of rocks on the opposite ridge overlooking the wagon train.

THREE

WAGONS WEST

Ira Gemmel and his partner Judas Beedon were simmering with indignation that their scheme to destroy the wagon train had gone awry. The two men were well known around the town of Santa Rosa in the Pecos Valley. Gemmel was the brains of the outfit and issued all the orders.

A stout dude, his short sight meant he had been forced to wear spectacles from childhood. Coupled with a portly constitution, he became the butt of school bullies. But young Ira was no milksop. A plan was devised to scotch the fun of the two main perpetrators. He bought some cake from the local baker and laced it with rat poison. By stealing the tasty comestibles from the apparently weak victim, the tormenters paid a deadly price.

Nothing was ever proven. And the incident was put down as an unfortunate accident. However, it was noteworthy that from there on, nobody bothered Ira Gemmel any more.

The fatal incident also had the consequence of determining the future course of the cunning youth's choice of profession. No back-breaking hard graft from dawn 'til dusk with little to show for it but a meagre pittance. There had to be far easier ways for an enterprising dude to make lots of dough and a name that resonated.

And so it came about.

The spectacles were a distinct advantage in business, establishing an image of fair play and dependability. His was an outwardly easy-going nature that concealed a ruthless streak. As a consequence, Ira Gemmel found no difficulty in gaining the confidence of those he planned to hoodwink.

If potential investors in his dubious schemes had been more observant, they would have been distinctly wary of the rather too broad a smile, the icy glint in his gaze and flaccid handshake. All were clear pointers that the guy should be given a wide berth. For most, however, it was too late before the gullible victims realized their mistake in trusting the devious trader.

That was how he had managed to become top dog in Santa Rosa.

His associate was a thin faced weasel of shifty character. Unkempt in appearance in total contrast to the well-groomed businessman, Judas Beedon was rarely in evidence when deals were struck.

The little guy's real name was Ezra. He had

acquired the biblical moniker after stealing thirty-one silver dollars from the cash box in the store where he and his younger brother Jethro worked. That was back east in the Missouri town of Kearney. After hiding the money, Ezra slipped the odd coin into Jethro's pocket.

The crime was soon discovered by the proprietor and the two brothers were immediately searched. Jethro Beedon was apprehended. Slow on the uptake, he failed to understand that his double-crossing kin was the real thief. The inevitable result transpired. Jethro was fired and given a sound thrashing for his disloyalty. A spell in the local hoosegow was passed by the circuit judge.

The ease with which the heinous skulduggery was accomplished made crime seem a far more lucrative prospect than hard graft for the duplicitous elder Beedon. He also headed west in search of adventure and easy pickings.

A loose tongue in a saloon revealed the ease with which his first crime had been committed and led to him being labelled a Judas. The name had stuck. Far from being overawed by the disgrace of his infamy, Judas relished the excitement and notoriety it brought.

The law was soon knocking at his door and Beedon was forced to flee. But not before the town marshal paid the ultimate penalty. Heading further west, Judas launched himself into a life of crime. He had shot and killed his first man. Marshal Zak Plenty was not to be his only victim.

The pair of villains had met up in Santa Rosa. They say that opposites attract. That was certainly the case with Gemmel and Beedon. The two n'er-do-wells hit it off from the start. They operated as a good team with Beedon supplying the muscle when it was required.

The fire-raisers mounted up and followed the course of the wagon train.

'Too bad that blaze the boys started hasn't worked out like you intended, Ira,' Beedon grunted. 'So what do we do now?'

Gemmel had been wondering that himself. 'We'll have to figure out some other way to stop that train getting to Santa Rosa,' he snarled out. 'I want it wiped out along with every last one of those damned settlers.'

The pursuers kept well back. They had no wish to become embroiled in the conflagration themselves.

All the two men could do now was tail the wagons as they fled before the advancing flames. With gritted teeth, Gemmel urged the charging conflagration onward almost as if it had taken on human form.

'Come on you bastard fire, catch them skunks and do your worst before they reach any water.'

From his position high up on the ridge, Gemmel could hear the panic-stricken shouts and hollers urging the wagon teams onward. Already tired after five weeks on the trail, the weary horses laboured under the cracking whips. Some were able to pick up the pace and outrun the raging firestorm. Others were not so lucky.

Jim Claymaker and Griff Reed raced back and

forth. Sweating in the grim heat that was drawing ever closer, they encouraged the drivers to greater efforts. The army scout knew that once they had crossed the Canadian River, the fire would quickly burn itself out with no more fuel to power its life force. But that was no consolation to the wagons at the rear that were struggling to keep up the frantic pace.

With moments to spare the leading wagons trundled across the shallow waters of the Sublette Narrows. Griff Reed counted them across.

'There's one missing, Jim,' he called out through the dense pall of smoke. 'It's Jake Sangster and his boy. One of their horses has thrown a shoe. So they were unable to keep up with the others.'

Sore eyes desperately tried to penetrate the searing fog. It was Claymaker who spotted the straggler. 'There it is!' he yelled out. 'And they're in bad shape.'

The stricken wagon burst out of the holocaust into full view. The fire had caught hold of the canvas awning and was threatening to devour the whole wagon and its occupants. The two men splashed across the flowing spread of the Canadian.

'Cut the traces, Jake, and set the horses free,' Reed shouted, his guttural holler seeking to penetrate the general din.

'All my goods are in this wagon,' the settler balked. 'I can't abandon everything.'

'Stay there and you'll get eaten up by the flames, yuh durned fool,' rapped the wagon master. 'Think of young Tom. You can always start up again. Where there's life there's hope. Stick with the wagon and you

29

ain't got a hope in hell.'

'Pop's right, Mister Sangster,' Claymaker added in support of his comrade. 'Cut the traces and I'll carry you and the boy to safety.'

'Don't forget that we're carrying another passenger,' Sangster reminded the leader. 'That woman we picked up in Walsenburg who needed a ride. She agreed to do the cooking and daily chores until we reach Cimarron.'

'I'll carry her out,' Reed said spurring his horse around to the rear of the wagon. 'Now let's get to it else the whole caboodle will flare up in our faces.'

Cut free the four horses needed no coercion to make a dash for the opposite bank of the river. As the army scout positioned Blaize beside the front seat of the wagon, Jake Sangster stepped across behind the rider while his son sat in front. They were only just in time. The schooner was now fully ablaze. But at least the river had halted the unrestrained march of the fire.

Claymaker anxiously threw a glance to where his old associate had disappeared behind the far side of the wagon. Heart in mouth, he waited in mid-stream ready to dive in should the need arise. Then he saw them emerging from the dark pall of smoke. Reed had grabbed up a sheet and soaked it in water before tossing it over their heads as protection against the clutching tongues of flame.

'I got her, Jim,' the wagon master declared, 'and she's OK.'

The wagon was anything but. It drifted away downstream, now a raging inferno.

'You were lucky, Mister Sangster,' Claymaker apologized. 'I'm just sorry we couldn't save any of your goods.'

The settler brushed off the regret. 'Our lives are more important than any meagre possessions,' he gasped out while holding firmly to the broad back of his saviour. 'It's like Pop said. Because of you guys, we can always start up afresh. Me and Tommy have a lot to thank you for. Not forgetting Miss Stapleton, of course.'

For a moment, mention of the passenger's name did not register with the scout. The on-going traumatic events were uppermost in his thoughts. Then it dawned. An astonished look was arrowed across towards the woman clinging on behind Pop Reed. Her face was hidden by a large bonnet. Could this really be Lavinia? If so, what was she doing on this wagon train?

Claymaker would have to curb his impatience for the time being.

The main priority was to ensure that the surviving prairie schooners and their occupants were safe; and the fire had been stopped in its tracks. Once he had dropped the Sangsters off on solid ground, the scout spurred away downstream. His aim was to track the burning wagon to ensure it did not beach on this side of the river. The tinder dry grass would only need a spark to ignite and quickly take a hold.

He was in luck. It had drifted across to the far side. After making sure it posed no further danger, Claymaker returned to the train where he was

31

anxious to seek out the mysterious lady who had accompanied the Sangsters.

Pop Reed was busy arranging the wagons into a circle. 'This seems as good a spot as any to make camp for the night,' he declared snapping out orders to the various wagon elders. 'These folks have had more than enough excitement for one day. Guess we could all do with a bite to eat and some rest.'

'What's happened to Jake Sangster and his boy?' enquired the scout.

In reality he wanted to know the whereabouts of Miss Stapleton. But diving straight in with such an enquiry would likely occasion more interest than he was prepared to explain. This was a distinctly private matter, and he wanted to keep it that way. Any talk of mail-order brides with a traditional guy like Pop Reed could be embarrassing.

'Abel Steward and his wife have taken them on until we reach Cimarron,' Reed elucidated while directing operations. 'Jake was sensible enough to take out insurance so he'll be able to buy a new wagon and supplies to continue the journey down to Santa Rosa. That's where all these good folks hope to settle down.'

Before Green River could pose his own query, a burly well dressed dude stepped forward. Unlike the other settlers, he was clad in a store-bought blue suit and necktie. 'All except me,' announced the man holding out a hand. 'The name is Fletcher Mason. I'm a lawyer from West Virginia. I've come west in search of a man called Bart Travis. You don't happen to know of him by any chance, do you, sir?'

Claymaker accepted the proffered hand. He pondered over the query for no more than a moment. 'The name don't mean anything to me. What about you, Pop?'

'Me neither,' said the wagon boss. 'You already asked me that question before, Mason. What's this guy done to have brought you all the way out here?'

Mason's attitude stiffened. 'That is something that I do not wish to divulge,' he stressed. 'Being a lawyer, my reputation depends on trust and confidentiality. I'm sure you understand. It would be unfortunate indeed if'n Travis were to hear about this business second hand.'

Eager to change the subject, Mason turned to the newly arrived army scout. 'How do you figure this fire started, Mister Claymaker?'

The scout had been mulling over that conundrum himself. 'Natural causes maybe. In summer these things are liable to flare up any place where there's enough tinder to catch alight. There again, it could be that some dude was careless with his cigarette end, or a discarded bottle.' His face hardened. 'If'n that's the cause, I'd sure like to catch up with the lunkhead that started it. A good friend of mine lost his life back there due to this fire. I ain't about to forget that in hurry.' Then he turned to Pop Reed. 'Perhaps you could arrange for the body to be collected and stowed in the supply wagon.'

The wagon master nodded. He then instructed one of the men to ride into the Costilla to the place described by Jim Claymaker. With a whole heap of other folks milling about seeking advice and help from the boss, Claymaker was forced to bide his time regarding his own personal problem.

Much as he had scanned the faces in the immediate vicinity, there was no sign of the illusive Miss Stapleton. Perhaps she had gone down to the river's edge to freshen up, or was resting up in one of the wagons. Again the dilemma flooded his brain as to what she was doing on the train.

Only when the evening meal had been served did the opportunity present itself. The two men were hunkered down, backs against a wagon wheel smoking cigars. Choosing his moment, Jim Claymaker tentatively raised the all-important question. 'What happened to Miss Stapleton? Ain't seen her around since she was rescued.'

'The Smiths have taken her in,' replied an unwitting Pop Reed. 'Poor gal was so shaken up after that fracas, she went straight to sleep in back of their wagon.'

'Maybe I should check up on her,' posed the nervous suitor. 'Seems only right after all that upheaval, and seeing as she's lost all her goods.'

'Be my guest, Jim,' responded the wagon master whose immediate concerns were taken up with bedding down his charges for the night. 'Their wagon is that one over yonder.' An arm vaguely pointed out the appropriate Conestoga.

Without any further discussion, Jim Claymaker rose to his feet. A gentle sigh of relief trickled from between pursed lips that his associate had not sought to further probe his interest in the lone female traveller.

Ambling across the central arena of the enclosed wagon circle, he nodded to various people. Acknowledgements for their gratitude regarding the assistance he had provided during the burning calamity were briefly accorded. The main focus of his attention was how to approach the problem of Miss Stapleton. If indeed it was a problem. He paused outside the appropriate wagon.

A man was greasing the wheel hubs of his wagon while his wife cleared up the remnants of their evening meal. Hank Smith looked up.

'Ain't thanked you for all your help earlier,' the settler stated. 'That sure was one nasty shock for us all. Don't suppose you've any notion yet as to what caused it?'

Claymaker shook his head. He did not really want to split the breeze with the guy.

But civility demanded he engage in some brief verbal exchange before posing the true reason for his visit. Accepting a mug of coffee, he made an excuse about checking that each wagon was still serviceable following the mad dash to escape the firestorm.

'Nothing that can't be put right with a pot of grease,' replied the pragmatic teamster eager to daub another generous dollop of the sticky mixture on to the moving parts of the wagon. 'Too many wagons have come to grief owing to a lack of adequate greasing. Always take a large pot wherever I go.'

'Glad to hear it,' Claymaker asserted. 'You can't be too careful.' A cough ostensibly to clear his throat summoned up the nerve to submit the imperative query concerning the Smiths' mysterious passenger. 'Pop tells me that you've taken in the woman he rescued from the Sangsters' burning wagon.' Observing the settler's quizzical frown, he hurried on. 'Seems like I might know her from some place,' the scout gingerly announced. 'But she ain't been seen since.'

'Poor dear was so drained after being rescued that she collapsed,' interjected Maud Smith. 'I put her to bed straight away.' The older woman slung a thumb towards the covered wagon. 'Me and Hank usually sleep out here under a canvas awning. It don't seem right to disturb the girl after all she's been through. Best leave her be.'

So that was that. Claymaker stifled a grunt of irritation. No chance of assuaging his curiosity yet awhile. He would have to wait until the morning before determining if she was the woman he had selected from the proscribed catalogue. Making his excuses, the scout moved off presumably to visit the other wagons.

Circling around, he made his way back to the site where the wagon master had set up his own night camp.

Reed was delegating responsibility for the regular four-hour watch system to a young guy who had offered his services for the duration of the trek. Billy Joe Winder had expressed a yearning to learn the craft of wagon train organisation. Ever ready to encourage youthful enterprise, Pop was more than willing to foster the kid's enthusiasm. Not having to pay out any wages was also a poignant incentive.

He issued his orders as to the teamsters standing guard that night. Billy Joe hurried off leaving the two men to chew over the traumatic events of the day.

FOUR

BAD FOR
RUNNING BEAR

After the wagon train had made camp, the two schemers were forced to cool their heels on the ridge overlooking the circle. They could not do anything until darkness had fallen. Settling down on the blind side, a low murmur drifted up from the camp below as the pioneers made themselves comfortable.

'No smoking!' Gemmel snapped as his confederate made to light up. 'Do you want to alert those critters to our presence up here?'

Gemmel had learned early on in life to curb his impatience. Not so Judas Beedon who was straining at the leash. He was eager to set the next part of any scheme dreamed up by his partner in motion. The boss man chopped his mumbled complaint off short with an angry glower.

'You never learn, do you Judas?' the trader snorted disdainfully. 'Patience is a virtue you'd do well to heed. Rushing in without careful planning will always end in disaster. We stay up here until its dark. Only then will it be safe to sneak down there and learn something to our advantage.' His eyes narrowed to thin slits as past events nagged at his memory. 'It's taken me two years to build up the business in Santa Rosa. So I ain't about to let those varmints spoil my pitch.'

Beedon merely grunted in reply. His rodent-like face crinkled in perplexity. 'So why are you so all riled up with this particular group of settlers? Starting a range fire is serious business. They must have done something real bad to have put you in such a blamed ornery temper.'

Gemmel's ruddy face bubbled with undiluted hatred. He shook an angry fist towards the settler camp then threw a cautionary look at his confederate. 'That's my business. I ain't about to divulge my reasoning to anybody until I'm good and ready. Especially the hired help.'

An abusive putdown of that nature irked the little man. 'Just cos I ain't got your gift of winning over people with a silky tongue don't mean you can treat me like some lowlife varmint.' Beedon was fuming. He lurched to his feet, fists clenched. 'Without my help, you'd never have got where you are today. I'm your right-hand man and don't you forget it. We're partners in this caper.'

Gemmel urged him to calm down. But he also

understood that he had gone too far.

Quickly the devious trader sought to backtrack. A fervent assurance was given of his need for the weasel's valuable contribution to the spread of their activities.

'Of course we're partners. I know that, Judas,' he assured his colleague in a more conciliatory tone. 'It was just my irritation overriding things. But don't worry. When the time is right, you'll be the first to know the whole story.'

As always, the ready smile and playful slap on the back assuaged Beedon's resentment. Just like it had those dupes who had failed to properly read the small print on the loan contracts they had signed.

Eventually the moment arrived when the two tricksters could emerge from hiding. Luck was on their side. A full moon provided enough light to guide their passage down through the rocks and undergrowth. A gentle breeze rustled the branches of ponderosa pine trees effectively concealing any sound of their descent. But ever the cautious operator, Gemmel still urged due care to avoid any unwelcome sound.

The bottom of the slope was reached without mishap. Gingerly, both men crept towards the circle of wagons ensuring they remained just outside the light cast by the cooking fires. From there, they began slowly to move around the outer edge.

When anybody was close by, they paused. Gemmel then listened in to the various conversations. His hope was to pick up some snippet of information that would provide the channel through which to further his deadly plan of destruction.

Most of the talk was mundane and of no interest to the skulking listeners. Some were discussing the fire and how lucky they were to have survived. Gemmel smiled to himself. There was no indications mooted that the cause of the blaze had been anything but an accident. One of those hazards that could flare up at any time.

After half an hour of listening in to boring chitchat, Beedon was again becoming restless. 'This ain't no use,' he grumbled. 'And hearing folks talk about what they're having for supper has made me realize I'm darned hungry.'

'Keep your voice down,' Gemmel hissed out knowing that raised voices carried at night. His terse response was guarded yet delivered in an urgent whisper. 'And don't forget. Everything comes to him who waits. Sooner or later we'll strike gold.'

And that was just what happened.

They were half way round the circle when Gemmel noticed three figures sitting beside a fire and smoking cigars. Two were clad in buckskins while the third was a snappily dressed dude.

Gemmel's back stiffened. Recognition of the younger man was instant. The long black hair and brown stetson with an eagle feather stuck in the hat band were a dead giveaway. His face distorted into a hard grimace of aversion. So why had Jim Claymaker tied up with the wagon train?

'We need to move in closer and listen in to their

41

conflab,' he whispered to his accomplice. 'This could be our big chance.' Careful not to make a sound, the two watchers soon came within hearing range.

The talk was all about the following day's travel. Pop Reed had decided to take the longer route to avoid any chance of becoming trapped in the Costilla Valley should another fire break out. 'Trouble is that we'll have to cross Indian land,' he sighed furrowing his brow in thought. 'And that's under the control of Yellow Knife.'

'Is he likely to challenge our passage?' enquired Fletcher Mason.

'He's the main chief of the southern Comanche tribe,' butted in Claymaker. 'Normally he's a fair-minded redskin. But with all these settlers heading west, Yellow Knife has become a mite touchy about them crossing his land. He's worried that they'll decide to stay. And that could scare off the buffalo.'

'Indians depend on those big woollies for every-thing – food, clothing, tepees, the lot,' added Reed. He arrowed a critical look at his old buddy. 'And the army ain't helping by encouraging hunters to shoot 'em down.'

Claymaker ignored the half-hearted jibe. 'I heard tell Broken Lance has sought refuge with Yellow Knife after we lost him back in the spring. You know any-thing about that, Pop?' asked Claymaker tipping a generous slug of whiskey into his coffee mug. It helped keep out the evening chill that often occurred under clearing skies in the summer time.

'The chief is Broken Lance's uncle. But he's not

one to invite trouble if'n it can be avoided. So far he's kept the hotheads in the tribe, including Broken Lance, under a close rein.'

'Then let's hope it stays that way,' commented Mason. 'I need to reach Santa Rosa soon to conclude my business.'

Pop Reed balked at the somewhat egotistical comment. 'If'n you ask me, I reckon the safety of all these good folks is sight more important than any business deal you have going, Mason. And the chief is growing old. How long he can continue to hold the hotheads in check is anybody's guess.'

'No offence meant,' the lawyer apologized. 'All I meant was that we all want to get through this in one piece.'

Not wishing to exacerbate any friction between the two men, Claymaker suggested a possible solution to their having to take the longer route. 'I've had dealings with Yellow Knife in the past. He accepted the agreement last year that guaranteed his tribe extra rations during the winter months when pickings are lean. Reckon I can persuade him that this train won't cause no trouble. What d'you reckon, Pop?'

'Sounds good to me,' the old buzzard concurred.

'I'll set off at first light then.'

And with that, the three men turned in for the night.

Crouching in the bushes behind the supply wagon, Gemmel turned to his accomplice. 'It's a stroke of luck Claymaker being with the train. Now I can get even with the skunk for spoiling that deal I had selling

meat to the army. He claimed it was unfit for dogs.'
An ugly snarl rumbled in Gemmel's throat. 'This is my
big chance to put the kibosh on that skunk's plan.'

As the two watchers slunk away, Beedon was having
second thoughts.

He was well aware of Jim Claymaker's reputation
for fair play and doggedly pursuing miscreants who
crossed his path. The meat debacle had been a case in
point. They had only escaped the full rigour of the
law by the skin of their teeth. And that was all down to
a fancy lawyer quoting the small print in the contract
enabling them to wriggle out of a conviction.

'I don't know, Ira,' he muttered hesitantly. 'Going
up against Claymaker could be bad news. You can
count me out if'n. . . .'

'Shut your mouth!' Gemmel's waxy rasp choked off
the weasel's bleating. 'I'm making the decisions here.
And I ain't about to throw this chance away. We need
to persuade Yellow Knife that those settlers caused the
range fire and they need to be stopped. He can do
that for us.'

Beedon was still not convinced. 'Yellow Knife ain't
too partial to us, Ira, after we sold him those dud car-
tridges for the rifles last fall.'

Beedon's uneasy timidity was beginning to vex the
trader. A grunt of irritation gurgled as he snapped out
a terse reposte. 'And didn't we show him that it was all
an unfortunate mistake by exchanging them for good
ones? Those old Springfields the army threw out
netted us a handsome profit. And Yellow Knife was
well satisfied with the deal.'

Beedon had to accept that they had indeed done well from that exchange.

Gemmel then went on to consolidate his reasoning. 'He needs us just as much as we need him. The furs and hides he hands over in exchange for trade goods help keep you in the finest Scotch whiskey.'

After returning to where they had concealed their horses, the two villains mounted up. Gemmel needed to reach the Indian camp on the far side of Cordova Pass before Claymaker, and that meant a night ride.

The moon was still high in the sky. Its ethereal glow lit their way across the uneven terrain. Pools of silvery radiance imbued a strangely hypnotic allure to the journey. To Ira Gemmel it was a bonus offering a clear trail to follow. But to his superstitious partner, every dark shape was transformed into a sinister denizen waiting to ensnare its prey. As the white orb made its way across the black firmament, Beedon became edgier than a Mexican jumping bean.

Gemmel thoroughly enjoyed the little guy's discomfort, purposely intensifying his fears with ghostly comments. Only when the sky clouded over and they stopped to make camp was Beedon able to relax.

'Never figured you for a weak-kneed rookie who believed in ghosts,' Gemmel mockingly derided his associate. 'Believing in all that stuff is for the fairies.'

'My ma used to tell fortunes with a crystal ball and she was often right in her predictions,' countered the Judas vigorously. 'Laugh at things you don't understand, Ira, and fate will make you pay for it.'

'Load of hogwash if'n you ask me,' came back the sneering rebuke. Although it was noteworthy that he held his tongue after that. Frequent wary looks were cast towards the darkest corners of the glade in which they were camped.

Both men were more than relieved to set off next morning. The golden ball rising above the scalloped moulding of the Sangre de Cristos Mountains was never more welcome. Their route into the Comanche stronghold was through a rough scrabble of rocky terrain. Even though there was no discernible trail to follow, both men knew the way having made the trip numerous times before.

Trading with the Indians was a major part of Ira Gemmel's business interests. And not only trade goods were exchanged. Gold and silver had been discovered on Comanche tribal land. The yellow peril, so precious to the hated white invaders, was of little value to the Indians. Just one more reason for Yellow Knife's distrust of the white eyes. But Gemmel had been able to secure a regular supply from the Indians for very little outlay. It was a lucrative arrangement he had no intention of forfeiting.

They had reached a plateau overlooking a stretch of broken land to their left when Judas Beedon's hawkish gaze noticed a movement down below.

'Somebody is heading this way, Ira,' he hissed pointing to the lone rider. 'And it looks like the chief's son, Running Bear.'

Gemmel's good eye squinted as he followed his partner's directive. 'By hokey, you're right.'

'What in tarnation is he doing out here?' questioned Beedon.

'Looks like the kid's been hunting. But who cares?' Gemmel's eyes glittered as a cunning ploy leapt into his brain. 'This could be our chance to fix things good and proper so Yellow Knife don't need no persuading to attack the wagon train.'

'What do you have in mind, Ira?'

'Pull back out of sight,' Gemmel ordered, drawing his pistol and checking the load. 'The way he's going, he'll pass close by in another ten minutes. That's when we take him out.'

Beedon's eyes popped. Ever the wary cynic, he voiced his concern vehemently. 'You're gonna kill the son of a Comanche chief? You sure that's the right thing to do? If'n it goes wrong, we're in big trouble.'

Gemmel scoffed. 'Of course I'm sure. Didn't figure you for a spineless wimp, Judas. But if'n you lack the backbone, I'll do the job myself.'

'That ain't fair, Ira,' protested Beedon. 'Ain't I always been there to back your play before? But how is killing the kid gonna help us?'

'I'm aiming to make Yellow Knife think it was Claymaker who did the dirty deed.' Gemmel chuckled uproariously at his deadly ploy. 'He's gonna be so riled up, those skunks from Concordia won't stand a chance once he hits the warpath.'

'You gotten a plan to ensure those critters take the rap?'

'Of course I have, you turkey,' Gemmel scoffed. 'We'll head direct for the Indian camp and tell Yellow

Knife exactly what happened. Only difference will be that we'll change the names.'

Beedon nodded as the penny dropped. 'I get it. Claymaker instead of Gemmel and Beedon.'

'Exactly,' leered Gemmel. 'You're catching on fast, Judas. So are you in?'

'Of course I am. But we haul off together and make certain the kid don't get up.'

Gemmel nodded then peered out from the cluster of rocks behind which they were concealed. 'Another two minutes and he'll be passing the other side of these rocks.'

Totally unaware that his life was in danger, Running Bear trotted along happily. The carcase of a deer was strapped to his back. Gemmel's horse whinnied at the crucial moment alerting the young brave to his peril.

Running Bear looked round. He saw the two killers bearing down on him. Dark eyes widened as recognition took hold. The treacherous gun runners were playing him false.

From an early age, Comanche youngsters were taught to react instantly to danger. Bare heels jabbed into the flanks of the mustang to escape this unexpected threat. The pony leapt forward just as the two bushwhackers closed in. Running Bear leaned over the side of his horse to present a smaller target.

Two pistols roared. One bullet ricocheted off a rock inches from the young brave's head. But the second struck the horse in the neck. The animal pitched forward throwing the Indian off. He tumbled down a rough slope and over the edge of a steep sided gulch.

The dull thud as he hit the hard ground below reached the ears of the gunmen. They quickly hurried across to the lip of the ravine and scrutinized the still form for any signs of movement. There was none. His head was covered in blood where it had struck a rock.

But Gemmel wanted to make certain the kid was dead. Unfortunately there was no easy way down into the gulch for a closer check. So he pumped another two slugs down. The callous disregard for life was rewarded as blood poured from a wound.

Still no indication that any life remained.

'Looks like he's a goner, all right,' observed Beedon holstering his own pistol. 'The fall together with those .45 shells did for him.'

'No time to hang around here then,' the trader retorted mounting up. 'We need to reach Yellow Knife's camp and tell him the awful news.'

'I'll practice some weeping and wailing on the way to make it look good,' snorted Beedon blurting out a series of ululating lamentations.

'Don't make it sound too heart-rending.' Gemmel guffawed. 'Yellow Knife don't need to feel we're overly distraught or he might smell a rat.'

Hearty chuckles echoed back from the solid rock walls as they spurred off.

FIVE

GREEN RIVER DOWN

The two charlatans made good time across country and reached the cluster of Indian tepees around mid-morning of the following day. They drew to a halt on a ridge overlooking the camp. Nothing untoward appeared to have disturbed the tranquil calm embodied within the rustic scene. Gemmel issued a thankful sigh.

'All looks quiet. And that's how we want it,' he said. 'You never can tell with these red devils. Anything can launch them on some hair-brained rampage.'

'Well we're about to set the cat among the pigeons, that's for sure,' Beedon evinced. The croak in his voice betrayed a nervous disposition. 'Let's hope they don't take their anger out on us.' Now that they had finally arrived, the weasel was once again becoming a mite jittery.

'After we lay down the facts agreed on, and express our deepest condolences, those varmints will be eating out of our hands,' Gemmel emphasized, stifling his own qualms. 'They ain't gonna harm us. Yellow Knife needs us just as much as we need him. Both of us have benefitted from the trading exchanges. And we're the only guys on the frontier willing to sell him ammunition for those Springfields.'

Gemmel's upbeat manner appeared to satisfy Beedon. 'He'll also need us to lead him to where Running Bear's body was left.'

Gingerly so as not to invite any sudden retaliation against their intrusion, the two men nudged their horses down the slope.

The camp of Yellow Knife was situated on the banks of Grape Creek. The tepees had been erected in neat lines. Each was decorated with brightly coloured paintings of birds and animals. Geometric designs were also much in evidence. It was clear that this was not a temporary site. Fields of maize and beans had been planted to support the diet of buffalo meat.

Many animal skins could be seen stretched across frames drying in the sun. And numerous fires were being tended by squaws preparing the midday meal in smoking pots containing stewed meat.

Over to one side, a medicine man was extolling a group of youngsters with the importance of Mother Earth. From the moment they could walk, the notion was drilled into them that the natural environment should be respected. Everything had a dignity and importance of its own. Nothing was wasted.

In front of the chief's tepee, Yellow Knife bedecked in an elaborated headdress of eagle feathers, was holding forth to a council of elders. On spotting the newcomers riding in, everybody ceased what they were doing. The arrival of white men in the camp was always greeted with suspicion. An ugly murmuring broke out amongst the sullen watchers. Braves reached for their weapons. Hostile looks were arrowed at the approaching riders.

Only when they were close up did Yellow Knife recognize the two traders with whom he conducted regular transactions. Legs akimbo, arms crossed over his chest, the stoical chief awaited the incomers. An arrogant almost regal demeanour issued a challenge for the newcomers to state their business.

The chief voiced the thoughts that were in all their minds. 'What is the white trader and his weasel-faced associate doing here so soon after our last exchange?' Beedon stiffened. But he had the good sense to hold his counsel. 'The next batch of skins is not yet ready.'

Gemmel raised an arm in greeting. 'We come in peace, noble chief of the Comanche nation.' His head dropped, a doleful expression preparing the way for the bad news that had to be imparted. He swallowed, a nervous cough heralding the grim tidings. 'But this is not a visit that me and my partner wanted to make. We have witnessed an evil crime that involves your son Running Bear.'

Yellow Knife flinched. He gripped the ceremonial tomahawk tightly. Beedon recoiled. His face turned a paler shade of grey.

'What has happened that requires your presence here?' he punched out bluntly while brandishing the deadly weapon.

Gemmel's arms remained high. 'There was an argument between some of the white men from the wagon train camped near the Canadian River. They were out hunting deer. The man you know as Black Hair was with them. I do not know what it was about. Only that they met up with Running Bear and he was shot and killed.'

'We would have stopped them, but there were too many for us to handle alone,' Beedon added forcing a burbling sniffle in support of his apparent distress.

The chief's broad shoulders slumped as pure angst creased his leathery features. For a long minute he was lost in a world of pain and anguish. Yet ever the consummate tribal leader, he shrugged it off. A growl of anger rumbled in his throat. That was the sort of reaction expected from a strong leader, as would a brutal reprisal to avenge such a dastardly occurrence.

'Get a party of your finest braves together, chief,' purred Gemmel, eager to display a fitting empathy for the distraught Comanche. 'We'll take you to the place where it happened so you can retrieve the boy's body for burial.'

Around the same time, Jim Claymaker was setting off from the wagon train to seek out the Comanche leader. He was confident that his entreaty would have a successful outcome. Yellow Knife was a sensible leader not prone to irrational outbursts of violence.

That was in stark contrast to his wayward nephew, Broken Lance who was a reckless firebrand more than likely to stir up trouble.

'Good luck, Jim,' Pop Reed muttered in a somewhat less enthusiastic tone. 'I sure hope you know what you're doing. Yellow Knife is no pushover.'

'Don't worry about me, old timer,' Claymaker effused. 'I know how to handle these redskins. Reckon I can persuade him to allow the train through his land.'

'What happens if'n he don't play ball?' Fletcher Mason butted in. 'From what I here, the more hostile braves in the tribe have been causing ructions of late.'

'That notion don't bear thinking on, Mason.' Claymaker glared at the pessimistic lawyer. 'It's my neck on the line here. I'm prepared to take the risk to help you folks out. Fail in that and we all pay the price.'

Without another word he spurred off.

His trail was in the same direction as that followed by Gemmel and Beedon. But unbeknown to the intrepid army scout, he was on a collision course with destiny, the outcome of which he could never have anticipated.

A steady canter was established to conserve the appaloosa stallion's energy. It was a long ride to the Comanche camp in the heart of the Sangre de Cristos. Height was soon gained amidst the rolling foothills where the blue gramma grass of the plains surrendered to a cactus and sagebrush environment.

Ahead the terrain became ever more rugged as

befitted an Indian stronghold. Claymaker's military mind acknowledged the Comanche chief's astute choice of command centre. It was in a rocky enclave safe from any surprise attack.

Drawing close to the gulch in which Running Bear had suffered such an ignominious tragedy, he suddenly drew Blaize to a halt.

'Looks like we ain't the only one's to pass this way,' he murmured studying the horse tracks with a practiced eye. 'Two riders, and white men judging by the shod hoof prints.' Dismounting he bent down to examine the spore more closely. 'They stopped here for a spell, then moved over yonder to the lip of the plateau.' Lines of puzzlement creased his brow. The scout's suspicious nature took over. 'Now what could be so interesting that dragged those jaspers to the edge of a remote gulch? Only one way to find out.'

He peered over the edge of the steep incline, and immediately spotting the prone body of a young Indian brave. The dried blood caking the still form told of a violent confrontation, no doubt with the owners of the shod horses. The bloody carcase of a deer was draped across his back. And close by lay an Indian pony with a bullet wound in its neck. That confirmed his suspicions.

From his lofty perch Green River could see that there was no safe way down into the deep ravine. However, a brisk recce along the ridge brought him to a stone-chocked gully. With extreme care, it would be just possible for a horse and rider to reach the bottom. A sharp whistle summoned the faithful Blaize to his side.

'It's up to you from here on, old fella,' he remarked stroking the animal's proud head. 'Reckon you can do it?' A curt neigh of accord found the duo clambering down the steep rift with nimble dexterity.

Before he had chance to examine the apparently lifeless body, the drumming of hoofs caught his attention. Wheeling around he saw a band of Indians thundering down the gulch. In the lead were two white men.

In a trice he recognized Ira Gemmel and his rattish associate.

Gemmel pointed to the kneeling man. 'That's Claymaker!' he called out on impulse. 'He's with the wagon train.' A lurid grin spread across the reprobate's face. This was working out much better than he had hoped. 'And it looks like he's come back to get rid of the body so's it wouldn't be found. We arrived in the nick of time to catch the skunk red-handed.'

The scout was stunned by the sudden change in circumstances. Not least the fact that he was being accused of the killing. And from the grim scowl clouding Yellow Knife's cratered face, the chief was in no mood for excuses. Nonetheless, Claymaker was not slow in vehemently professing his innocence.

'This was not my doing, great chief,' he exclaimed. 'I found Running Bear like this and was going to . . .'

But Yellow Knife was immune to reasoning. He angrily waved the excuses aside.

'Take the treacherous killer,' he ordered his braves. 'He will suffer greatly for his crime. The slaying of my son will be avenged in true Comanche fashion. And it will be no easy death for you, Black Hair.'

'But I'm innocent, chief,' he protested vigorously. 'I found him like this and intended bringing him to your camp.'

Broken Lance was the first to step forward. 'Lies! Black Hair is only trying to save his own skin. Grab him, my braves.'

An ugly smile appeared on Ira Beedon's face. He stepped back allowing the hot headed Comanche bucks to take charge.

It was obvious that no amount of exhortations would sway the incensed chief's decision. But Claymaker was not prepared to be taken without a fight. Three braves rushed forward. They soon discovered that he was no soft touch. Fists slammed into the red faces driving them back. One buck tried diving on to his back but a slick twist of the hips saw the critter flying head over heels into a clump of cholla cacti.

That was when Broken Lance decided that a decisive hand was needed.

Seeing the rebellious Comanche smirking and eager to avenge his defeat at Coal Creek made the army scout see red. Without thought for his own safety, he lunged at the sneering buck. The attack took Broken Lance by surprise as Claymaker bore them both to the ground.

They rolled over in the dust. The Indian was the first to recover. He jumped up and caught a tomahawk tossed to him by a comrade. Waving it above his head he readied himself for the fatal sweep. The two adversaries circled each other warily. Howls of glee urged Broken Lance to finish off the hated white eyes quickly.

The Indian knew that he had to act boldly to maintain his status in the tribe. Following a few deft feints with the blade, he dived in. The deadly axe cut through the air. It would have cleaved the scout's head in two had he not twisted aside in the nick of time.

Broken Lance snarled. But Lady Luck was squatting on his shoulders. As the army scout backed away he tripped over a rock and tumbled into the dust.

A howl of triumph erupted from the Indian's open maw. 'You will not escape a second time, Black Hair.'

As the Indian came forward, Claymaker leapt to his feet and drew his revolver aiming the barrel at the advancing figure.

Ira Gemmel had spotted the move and knew that immediate action was required to prevent Claymaker winning the contest. The last thing he wanted was for the scout to wriggle out of this. Drawing his own pistol, he quickly stepped up behind. The butt crashed down on Claymaker's head. A burning flash of light exploded inside his head, then nothing but blackness as he slumped to the ground unconscious.

'That's cooked your goose, mister,' the devious trader muttered to himself.

'And raised our standing with the Indians too,' added Beedon.

Under normal circumstances, Yellow Knife was a

Comanche whose life was governed by honour and fair dealing. But the heinous death of his son at the hands of the white eyes had soured his brain. His nephew had been right all along. None of the invaders could be trusted. All were tarred with the same brush. Black Hair was no better than any of the others.

The chief stood over the prone body, anger and hatred seeping from every pore of his being.

'Take the treacherous dog, my brave warriors,' Yellow Knife ordered. 'We will take him back to camp where all can enjoy his suffering for the base wrong he has perpetrated against our people.' A roar of approval burst from a dozen throats as the stunned army scout was manhandled on to his horse.

Gemmel nudged his partner. 'If'n this don't have these turkeys painted up and attacking that wagon train, then I'm a gopher's uncle.'

'Are we going along with them to enjoy the fun?' asked Beedon.

'Sure are,' Gemmel concurred. 'I want to see Claymaker's face when he wakes up. Then he'll know it's me that has him over a barrel this time. Nobody gets away with making a fool of Ira Gemmel.'

SIX

BURNING SPECTACLE

By the time the group of riders had reached the Indian encampment, Claymaker had recovered consciousness. His head was still fuzzy as the Indians dragged him off his horse. Two of them held him tight as Yellow Knife approached. The zealous chief had also regained his dignified bearing.

'So Black Hair,' the incensed chief snapped out. The deep resonance of his tone made the hairs on Claymaker's neck stand up. 'You are no better than all the other deceitful lowlifes of your kind. Peddling false promises and betraying those who foolishly placed their trust in your word.'

'I don't know what's made you figure I would perpetrate such a cowardly act,' the pinioned captive espoused with feeling. 'I say again, great chief, that I had no part in this crime. Haven't we always respected one another in the past? Remember it was I who persuaded the leaders of my people to supply you with winter feed when starvation was looming. Does that not prove I am an honourable friend of the Comanche?'

'Don't listen to him, Yellow Knife,' Gemmel interjected. 'He's the killer all right. I witnessed the foul deed with my very own eyes. And not only that. He's working for the wagon train. Isn't that so, Mister Beedon?'

'He's right, chief,' the Judas pontificated in an officious voice. 'Sure as eggs is eggs, this sidewinder killed Running Bear. No doubt about it. The critter was even laughing when he pulled the trigger.'

Claymaker's eyes bulged. He could scarcely believe what he was hearing. The moment of realization dawned that he was being framed. But why had they shot down Running Bear?

'You're lying, Beedon,' Claymaker snarled out as he struggled to escape the clutches of his Comanche guardians. 'So what game are you two rats playing?'

'No game, mister.' The devious trader turned to Yellow Knife, arms held aloft. 'Me and my partner only want to see justice done.' A look of pure virtue washed over the unctuous features, as if butter wouldn't melt in his mouth. 'You being in with the immigrants makes them equally to blame.' He shrugged apathetically. 'Far as I'm concerned Yellow Knife can do whatever he thinks fit. The great army scout has shown his true colours today. He has no thought for the Comanche and deserves to suffer a painful end for his treachery.'

So infuriated was Jim Claymaker that he made a concerted effort to break free. His sudden twists and writhing bore fruit. He dived at the vile face grinning at him. Gemmel was also caught out. A solid fist hammered at his jaw sending the trader sprawling back into his buddy. Both men tumbled over.

But Claymaker was not finished. He grabbed Gemmel by the shirt front. A sharp tearing of the material was ignored. 'I'll hammer the truth out of you for setting me up, Gemmel,' he howled ready to deliver some more punishment.

A left hook was ready to make its brutal contribution when the Indians recovered from the impulsive assault. A dozen rangy red men leapt on him and bore the writhing form to the ground. He didn't stand a chance. Sheer weight of numbers took their toll. Punches rained down on the exposed torso. Broken Lance made sure that he was well to the fore in dishing out the rigorous beating.

'Enough!' shouted Yellow Knife who was eager to seek recompense for his son's heinous death. 'Bring thongs to bind him firmly. We will stake the faithless cur out here and let him think long and hard on what lies in store for those who double-cross the Comanche.'

In vain the frontiersman tried to remonstrate. But Yellow Knife was immune to any pleas for clemency.

'My dead son now lies over in my tepee,' the chief railed, jabbing a finger towards the main tent. 'His mother and all our kin shed many tears of sadness. They are ready and eager to apply the torture of a thousand cuts to the killer. It is well. But not yet. That would be too quick an end. First you need to make peace with your own god and tremble at the fate awaiting those who dishonour our name.'

Yellow Knife paused to compose himself. Then he went on in a voice that shook with emotion. 'Soon we will attack the wagon train and make those invaders pay dearly for their infamy. Any that survive will be joining you in your torment. Only then will the soul of my son be consigned to the Great Spirit's care.'

Moving away from the victim, the chief issued his orders. There was much to organize before the war party could depart. Furious activity followed as braves gathered up their weapons. Axes and knife were sharpened. The Springfield rifles sold to them by Gemmel needed checking. Each brave was allotted a supply of ammunition.

Squaws were summoned to daub their men's faces with paint. A warrior believed that such adornment protected him in battle. These symbols told of his prowess in the field. The more he displayed, the greater was his bravery and success against the enemy. Legend stated that the predominantly red paint gave the Indian his name of red man amongst the immigrant European settlers.

Horses were the tribe's prize possessions. Amongst the Plains Indians, the Comanche were renowned as horsemen and revelled in exhibiting their dexterity. It was these skills that had made them a scourge of those who dared to defy their just right to these lands. The immigrants would soon taste the wrath of those they had so despairingly mortified.

When everything was ready, Yellow Knife summoned his braves. 'Before attacking the invaders,' he announced, 'we ride to the other villages and gather support from our brothers. The palefaces will then feel the full might of the Comanche nation.'

A roar of accord rose up as the braves hallooed and bawled. All were eager for the coming affray.

The two wily swindlers were standing to one side listening intently. 'This couldn't be working out better,' Gemmel muttered to his sidekick. 'We'll stick close to the Indians but make certain we ain't in the firing line when the fireworks start. But first I need to pay that skunk Claymaker a visit.'

The trader stalked across to where the scout was spread-eagled on the ground. Consciousness had returned. But his vision remained blurred making it a struggle to assimilate what had happened. A shadow blotted out the harsh rays of the sun as Gemmel stood over him.

The first thing he knew of the schemer's presence was a sharp jolt in his ribs from the toe of Gemmel's boot. Another two followed in quick succession. The scout winced but refused to cry out.

'That's something on account, Claymaker. But I'll be back once those accursed immigrants have been wiped out. And I'll enjoy watching these red devils work you over. And I'll be more than glad to lend them a helping hand.' Another searing barb lanced through the victim's helpless body. A final boot to the head made the scout see stars before he passed out. 'See you around, sucker.'

The evil perpetrator chortled uproariously then stamped away to join his partner.

Together they spurred after the Indian band. 'Now that Claymaker is out of the picture, nothing can stand in the way of my plan.'

Beedon eyed his partner quizzically. He still had no intimation of what Ira Gemmel's purpose was for seeking the destruction of this particular wagon train. And this was not the time to satisfy his curiosity.

Apart from one poignant observation.

'What happened to your specs?' he quizzed.

'That skunk Claymaker knocked 'em off when he attacked me.' He snarled at the recollection then gave a shrug of disdain. 'But I soon showed him who's boss.' The upbeat trader then removed a fresh pair of frames from his jacket. 'I always carry a spare set for emergencies. Now let's catch those redskins up.'

Back in the Comanche village, apart from a handful of stalwart guardians, only the old people together with women and children remained. Most were gathered around the chief's tepee. Inside, the tribal medicineman was carrying out the prescribed ritual of spiritual cleansing over the body of Running Bear. A sombre chant from the onlookers accompanied the bizarre ceremony. Hauntingly melodious, it was intended to ward off the influence of evil spirits. Meanwhile the shaman danced around the body wafting his arms in the prescribed manner.

Inveigling the whole fetid atmosphere was the pungent reek of buffalo dung smouldering in a central grate. Special purifying herbs were added to increase the potency of the funeral rite.

Swooping Owl, the boy's mother, sat close by rocking on her haunches. Her head was bowed in prayer to the great Manitou. Tears of grief dripped on to the sandy floor. A continual procession of mourn-ers joined the distraught squaw extolling their supportive empathy with a mournful lamentation.

Once he had delivered his eulogy, Big Bull, the medicine-man, donned the headdress and hide of a black bear to acquire the animal's aura. It was meant to signify that he possessed the power and influence over life and death.

Medicinemen were often highly intelligent with the gift of persuasive oratory. Their continued influ-ence and respect amongst the tribe, however, depended on success in the management of their duties. Failure in this respect could mean banish-ment. Big Bull had been the tribal priest and soothsayer for many years. His skills were legendary amongst the Comanche such that people came from far and wide to seek his wise counsel.

Lifting his arms towards the heavens, Big Bull stood over the prone form and intoned in sonorous monotone intended for the ears of Swooping Owl and her relatives.

'Running Bear is bound for a higher place. But the Great Manitou commands that his death will be avenged. The lodges of the Comanche will be graced by many paleface scalps when our heroic warriors return.' A graceful sweep of incense sticks passed over the prone body. 'Black Hair will be the last to die. And everyone in our village will participate in making his death the most memorable.'

And so it continued with Big Bull effectively preparing the way for the deceased youth's spirit to depart his earthly form.

The first thing that filtered through Claymaker's muzzy brain when he recovered consciousness for the second time was the discordant wailing from Yellow Knife's tepee. His head felt like it was being squeezed in a vice. He soon realized that his situation was dire in the extreme. Both arms and legs were staked out. Tightly knotted leather thongs ensured that he could barely move.

It was pretty obvious that Gemmel and his associate were responsible for Running Bear's death. And they had sneakily managed to pin the rap on to Claymaker and the wagon train. Although what was behind their heinous action remained a total mystery. Stuck in this perilous calamity, discovering the truth into which he had blundered was now impossible.

The captive struggled against the unyielding bonds, but to no avail. There was no way he could escape. Was this to be the final reckoning?

Green River Jim had been in some hairy situations during his varied career as a hunter and army scout. Battling renegade Indians, thieving merchants, grizzly bears, not to mention the harsh and unforgiving landscape. But nothing compared to his current predicament.

Yet ever the optimist, Claymaker forced his brain into a more buoyant outlook. Something had always turned up before when he found himself up against the odds.

Half delirious, he began muttering to himself.

Remember that time when you and Coyote were up in the Tetons hunting deer. A band of angry Shoshoni had trapped you both on a ledge of rock with no way out. The uneasy truce between white hunters and the native inhabitants had always been tenuous. Flare ups of violence could occur at any time. This was one such instance.

Within a short period, your ammunition had run out and the howling redskins were all set to rush your position. Two against fifty were not good odds. And with only knives to defend yourselves, the final count-down to oblivion was a sure-fired certainty. A shake of the hands and you both stood up ready to meet the rampaging Shoshini braves head on.

Then, all of a sudden, a jack rabbit emerged from a clump of bushes against the rock wall behind you. It scampered away. So where had it come from? Coyote had looked askance at you. Returning the puzzled frown a flash of inspiration struck you both at the same moment.

Scrabbling desperately at the bushes, a small hole was soon revealed. No more than two feet high, it was large enough to crawl inside where a tunnel soon resolved itself into an inner chamber. It was an old mine working. Long since abandoned, there had to be a proper entrance at the end of the passage.

An hour later and you were back in daylight. Certain death had been transformed by the miracle of an unwitting jack rabbit.

Could such a miracle be about to save Jim Claymaker's hide once again? He quickly shrugged off the threatened delusion. Frantic eyes scanned the immediate vicinity desperately seeking a way out of this dilemma. Then he saw something glinting in the pitiless hot sun.

Anxious peepers focused on to the lone object. It was a piece of glass. Then he remembered. A lens must have fallen out of Gemmel's spectacles when he had attacked the skunk before being restrained. And there it was, no more than a couple of inches from his left land. The steel frames lay apart, way out of reach. But could he stretch over to secure this valuable prize?

Here was his one and only hope of escaping and saving the good folks in the wagon train. An anxious look over to the tepee revealed that all the attention was directed towards comforting Running Bear's mother. Breath held in check, the tethered scout forced his hand over to where the glittering trophy sat winking at him. So near yet so far. Another inch and he would have it.

Girding up all his willpower, the reaching fingers stretched the leather thong to its very limit. For an instant the frantic scout feared that his chance of freedom had been callously snatched away. Then a single digit slid over the lens. Slowly, with infinite care, he dragged it back.

A sigh of relief issued from between gritted teeth. Taking a firm hold of the glass, he turned it round enabling the sun's rays to focus the heat on to the leather ties. It was an awkward and tiring process. Maintaining a static hand to keep the sun's fierce heat aimed at the one spot was extremely challenging.

It soon made his hand ache abominably. Teeth ground with a fierce intensity. Yet all he could do was persevere. Time appeared to pass at a snail's pace. Still nothing happened. The thong remained stubbornly intact.

Worried glances towards the tepee did not aid his concentration. Any second and somebody could wander across and decide to begin the threatened torment. Even though Yellow Knife had given orders that nothing should be done until his triumphal return, heartache and misery at the loss of a loved one can turn anybody's head.

Claymaker's attention returned to the task in hand. He had never been an avid follower of the Good News advocated by the bible. But now he prayed earnestly like he'd never done before.

Then suddenly, out of the blue, a whiff of smoke drifted up from the taut leather. Perhaps there was a God up there after all ensuring his welfare. He issued a silent plea of thanks. A dark brown singe mark appeared where the concentrated sunbeam had bored into the strip of hide. Slowly it grew bigger. The scout willed it onward. 'Come on, my beauty,' he urged frantically. 'You can do it.'

Pulling against the tough binder with all the strength he could muster, his acute hearing soon registered a tearing as the sinews began to part. In no time, his hand was free. After rubbing the bruised skin to get the blood flowing, he reached across and untied his other hand. Working swiftly, he struggled to his feet. Blaize was fastened to a picket line on the far side of the encampment.

He began moving across the open sward as silently as possible.

But that was when the good Lord decided that he had gone far enough. A little jinx needed to be tossed into the arena to stir things up. And it came in the form of a young brave who emerged from the tepee at the wrong moment. He saw the prisoner about to make his escape.

Arms flailing wildly he cried out, 'Black Hair has broken free. He is escaping.'

More Indians appeared all hollering and howling for his blood. 'Stop the paleface! After him before he can warn the wagon train.'

The scout stumbled. Stiffened muscles impeding movement refusing to do his bidding. He lurched awkwardly towards the place where Blaize was tethered. The faithful cayuse reared up on to his hind legs tugging at the picket line to break free.

The howling mob had smelt blood. They surged across the clearing and would be on him in no time. Was he after all to be denied the chance to save the immigrants? He cursed and railed at his impotence.

Then, at that very instant, the Good Lord decided it was time to intervene on his behalf. Fervent prayers had indeed been answered. Claymaker smiled. His eyes lifted to the heavens.

'You sure like playing games, don't you mister?' he mumbled under his breath.

SEVEN

RING OF DEFENCE . . .

Big Bull emerged from the tepee. His arms were raised towards the fermament. Invoking his most resonant and commanding voice, he proclaimed, 'The gods have seen fit to answer the pleas of Swooping Owl. Her revered son has return from the dead . . . Running Bear lives! Praise be to the Great Manitou.'

A murmur immediately rippled through the whole assembly. 'Running Bear lives! Running Bear lives! The gods have spoken.'

'Big Bull has once again shown that he is the greatest of healers.'

The medicineman acknowledged the adulation with a dignified bow. He was more than happy to revel in the glory and exaltation bestowed upon him. Excitement at this sudden yet welcome occurrence enveloped the whole camp. For a moment at least, the escape of Black Hair was forgotten as the crowd surged back into the tepee to witness this momentous feat of resurrection.

'Thank you, thank you.'

Grateful eyes were once again lifted skywards. Claymaker's silent expression of gratitude to his Maker found him able to stagger over to his horse. A supreme effort was required to haul his battered frame into the saddle. Without waiting to hear any more from the excited Comanches, he spurred off at the gallop. Soon enough they would remember. And then the fat would most definitely be in the fire.

Nevertheless, he was relieved that the chief's son was still alive. He recalled seeing two bullet holes in the deer carcase. That must have saved the kid's life. The true facts of the attempt on Running Bear's life would need to be related to Yellow Knife if the attack on the wagon train was to be prevented.

And that was the problem. The Comanche war party could already be engaged in their deadly reprisal.

There was no time to lose in heading back to where the train was encamped near the Canadian River. A surge of exhaustion threatened to overwhelm the scout as he pointed his horse in the direction of the encampment. It was a long ride. And there was not a moment to lose. Like the true army scout he was, Green River Jim shrugged off his inertia. The safety of the immigrants was more important.

He allowed Blaize to have his head. The trusty

74

appaloosa appeared to know instinctively the correct route to follow. Mountain terrain surrendered to arid plateau lands of sagebrush and mesquite. All were traversed in a somniferous blur. Claymaker was no stranger to napping in the saddle. Fatigue, however, was bound to catch up with even the most resolute of men.

As the spirited appaloosa climbed the winding trail up to the distinctive notch of Cordova Pass, Claymaker tumbled out of the saddle. It was clear that a rest was essential if he was to complete his task. Wrapping his weary frame in a blanket, the scout was asleep almost before his head touched the hard ground. Blaize stood guard over his master during the brief period of oblivion.

The new day announced its presence with a golden halo of ever-increasing brilliance. Rising in languid allure above the circlet of ramparts, its trenchant heat informed the waking catnapper that another hot one was in the offing.

A gulp of tepid liquid from his water bottle washed the foul taste out of his mouth. Limbs were stretched to ease out the stiffness. But there was no doubting, the sleep had done him a power of good. Blaize had also welcomed the brief respite. Fully refreshed, man and beast were soon bounding off on the final section of their journey.

Once the sandy wasteland of the Alamosa Flats was left behind, the rough foothill country descended gradually. And there below was the mighty Canadian slithering and squirming like a giant snake across the broad grassy plains.

The wagon train was easily spotted from afar. Smoke from numerous fires twisted up into the azure sky. A surge of relief rippled through tight muscles on seeing that the attack had not yet begun. But he had little misgiving that the threatened assault would not be far off.

The horse was urged to a pounding dash across the level ground.

Half way across, two men appeared from behind one of the wagons. The plume of dust in his wake had attracted their attention.

'That's Claymaker isn't it?' declared Fletcher Mason.

'Sure is,' replied Pop Reed stuffing the last of a cornbread muffin into his mouth. 'And he's going at too fast a gallop to be delivering good news.'

The scout hauled up in a swirling cloud of dust.

'Something wrong, Claymaker?' enquired Mason.

'Plenty!' the scout snapped back, leaping off his horse. 'Yellow Knife and his whole tribe are on the warpath. I was lucky to escape with my life. And its all on account of a skunk called Ira Gemmel.'

'I've heard tell of that jasper,' snorted Reed. 'And it ain't good. A right money-grabbing fraudster from what folks say. What's he been up to?'

In a concise summary, Claymaker described the startling events that had been played out since he left the wagon train four days before. By this time other members of the train had wandered across to find out what was happening.

The scout glanced over at them, his thoughts switching to the lady he still had not been able to locate. A brief scrutiny of the anxious faces told him she was not there. But this was not the time to resuscitate his private life. Pop Reed was already probing for more information on the double-dealing Indian trader.

'Why would that varmint want to set the Comanche on to our wagon train?' he queried, scratching a matt of tangled hair. 'I can understand why Yellow Knife might want revenge for his son being shot down by white men. But why would Gemmel urge him to do it?'

'I have a notion why the critter would have it in for me. We had some run-ins before,' iterated Claymaker.

'Yep,' agreed the wagon boss. 'As I recall, you kiboshed his plan to sell rancid meat to the army. That sure can't have made his day.'

'But you folks.' Claymaker shook his head in frustration. 'Don't make no sense to me. Is there anything unusual about this particular group of immigrants that makes them different? Something that would rattle Gemmel's cage.'

Reed shrugged his shoulders. He was completely baffled.

It was the lawyer who made a tentative suggestion. 'The only thing about these folks is that they're all from Concordia, Kansas. Although I can't see what that has to do with anything.'

'All that is except Miss Stapleton who joined us in Walsenburg,' said Reed. 'But she don't seem the type to be involved in any shady dealings. A right nice city gal from what I've seen of her. Said she needed to reach Cimarron to meet somebody.'

Claymaker was sorely tempted to press the wagon master for more information. But more critical matters regarding the imminent threat to life and limb were uppermost in his mind.

'Whatever his devious reasoning, we need to prepare for an attack.'

'I'll make sure all the men are armed and in position behind their wagons,' said Reed. 'I don't know what sort of weapons the Comanche have, but ours sure aren't the latest repeaters. These folks are farmers, not gunfighters. They only have some old Springfields.'

'I've spotted a few Ballards and Maynards around,' added Mason, eager to inform the frontiersmen that his knowledge extended beyond the compilation of pink-ribboned documents. 'And the guy over yonder has a Sharps Big Fifty. Those things can knock out a buffalo at one thousand yards.'

'You shoot as well as you talk, Mason?' prodded a sceptical Pop Reed.

The lawyer reached for the Hawken clutched across the wagon master's chest. 'Mind if'n I borrow this?' he asked, affecting a deliberately nonchalant mien.

'Be my guest,' smirked the old timer. 'It's loaded so mind how you go.' He threw a sceptical wink at Claymaker.

Mason licked his thumb and dragged it across the

front sight. Peering around he spotted a lone buzzard circling aloft in search of any abandoned foodstuff. Snapping the stock to his shoulder, the lawyer barely appeared to take aim when the long gun exploded. The bird plummeted to earth leaving both watchers open mouthed.

'Reckon he ain't all jaw after all, eh Pop?' commented a startled Green River Jim to his buddy. This guy might have been a wordsmith whose prowess was best exemplified in a court room, but he was no greenhorn, that was for sure.

The old boy shook his head in like wonderment. 'You ain't kidding there, Jim. I apologize for doubting you, Mister Mason.'

The lawyer nonchalantly acknowledged the contrition while handing the Hawken back to its owner. 'A nice weapon. But a mite too slow in the loading for me when the chips are down.'

'Where in tarnation did you learn to shoot like that, mister?' Pop blurted out.

'Lawyers need to get out of the office once in a while to check things out,' Mason replied. 'So a fella needs to be capable of defending himself in these uncertain times when bandits are likely to jump out from behind any rock on the trail. A lawman called Wild Bill Hickok taught me the rudiments. You might have heard of him.'

Claymaker and his buddy were well acquainted with the man and his reputation.

A couple of barking hounds fighting over the dead bird brought the trio back to the task in hand.

The lawyer further enhanced his new-found respect with the trailblazers by declaring, 'I've see a couple of guys with Henry repeaters. But they are only the dated 1863 models which have to be loaded at the muzzle end. And they looked a tad rusty as well.'

'What about Spencers?' asked Claymaker adding his contribution. 'They are more reliable than the Springfield, and less prone to jamming.'

'I agree,' nodded Reed having regained his composure. Mason stood to one side having made his contribution with astonishing effect. 'And the latest Spencer .45s have a tube magazine in the stock. But we ain't got any here.'

'Nothing can beat a Winchester though.' They all turned as Hank Smith spoke up. 'I bought the latest '73 model in Walsenburg. It was the last one on the shelf.'

'I'd like to see it sometime, Mister Smith,' Claymaker interjected. Although his request was merely an excuse to find out more concerning the Smiths' newly acquired passenger.

'Drop by the wagon anytime, Jim,' enthused the settler. 'You can try it out.'

'Much obliged. . . .' The tough scout paused, swallowing as he quickly formulated the words of his next sentence. 'I was also wondering how Miss. . . .'

But he never got to express the matter that was uppermost in his mind. Maud Smith chose that moment to interrupt the male-dominated discourse.

'What about us women, Pop?' she spouted firmly, hands resting defiantly on her ample hips. 'Seems to me that you're gonna need back-up. Folks to load the spare weapons ready to repulse them savages. No sense in you fellas wasting time. We could do all that. Ain't that right, ladies?' There was a positive murmur of agreement from the bonneted wives and daughters of the pioneers.

'And we'll need water if'n they loose off fire arrows,' shouted out another feisty dame from the rear. 'And don't forget some of you might get hit. Us gals have become well used to doctoring while we've been on the trail.'

Not one to harbour misgivings where female help was concerned, Reed willingly accepted the assistance being offered. He proceeded to give last minute instructions for all the gaps between the wagons to be filled in with baggage and boxes.

Claymaker scanned the anxious faces, once again searching for the illusive Lavinia Stapleton. He only had a single sepia-tinted print to aid his recognition. Was that her standing at the rear of the gathering? Piercing eyes narrowed trying to match the image to reality. He couldn't be sure. And had she recognized him?

No further time was afforded for idly speculating on either premise. The opportunity to investigate was suddenly terminated when a voice from the far side of the encampment cut through the general babble.

'Indians! They're here!'

Claymaker and the wagonmaster hustled over to where the redskins had been spotted. They were accompanied by Fletcher Mason. A line of Comanche warriors sat their horses along the ridge. Lances, rifles and bows were clearly on display. And it was obvious from the paint daub on their faces that this was not a social call.

'There's more of the critters over here,' sang out another tremulous voice from the opposite side of the wagon circle. 'They're all over the darned place.'

'By hokey!' Pop Reed exclaimed. 'We're surrounded.'

The stoical announcement was greeted by a collective sharp intake of breath. The scent of fear quickly rippled through the nervous pack.

'And it looks like the whole Comanche nation is out there,' observed Hank Smith.

Never one to panic when placed under pressure, Pop Reed quickly took control. 'Get all the kids under cover beneath the wagons,' he ordered in a firm yet measured tone. Inside he was quaking nervously. 'Then grab your weapons and cover every approach. Last thing we need is them breaking through.'

'What are they doing just standing up there on the ridge?' enquired Mason. 'Why don't the varmints swarm down here and attack?'

'That's an old ploy,' said Claymaker, 'to make us sweat. We sure aren't going any place so they're in no hurry.' He pointed to a tall brave sporting a splendidly beaded headdress encompassed by eagle feathers. The fiercesome warrior was also clad in a fine elaborately decorated buckskin jacket and breeches. 'That's Yellow Knife, their chief. As soon as he removes that head gear and jacket, we'll know that the time has come to defend ourselves.'

'Looks like a heap of them have Springfields,' commented Reed. 'I wonder where they bought those?'

Claymaker snorted. 'That has to be Gemmel's doing. I know for a fact that he snapped up a load that were being thrown out when the army exchanged them for the new Spencer .45s.'

A low yet insistent chant interrupted the scout's conviction. It slowly progressed around the enclosing Comanche circle rising to a shrill bleat. The ululating wail was intended to intimidate their foe. Accompanied by a steady throb as the braves beat their weapons against shields, its effect was blood curdling. Stifled cries of fear rose from a myriad throats as the settlers realized what they were up against.

Claymaker knew that panic had to be squashed if they were to succeed in repulsing the imminent assault. There was one chance that could avert the catastrophe. But it would need to be done immediately. Yellow Knife would only hold off for so long before launching his braves down the surrounding slopes. As long as he still wore the regalia of his high office, the prospect of preventing bloodshed remained.

'I'm going out there to negotiate with Yellow Knife,' he announced to the wagon master. 'There's a chance I can persuade him to back off.'

'You crazy?' Reed hollered out. 'Soon as he sees who's coming out to parley, your life won't be worth a plugged nickel. You've escaped his clutches, tossed dirt in his face. So he'll need to save face. No chief could allow that to go unchallenged. You'll be putting your head in the lion's mouth, Jim boy.' The old teamster gripped his friend's arm urging caution. 'The odds are stacked against you. Like as not you won't even get the chance to tell him that his son is still alive.'

Claymaker knew that Pop was right. He was certainly putting his life on the line. But what other choice was there? The immigrants were heavily outnumbered. Most of their weaponry was archaic. And it was obvious that Yellow Knife had been drumming up support from the other Indian encampments.

And he had been successful. There was a veritable hoard out there all eager to avenge the shooting of Running Bear, not to mention the paleface invasion of their hunting grounds.

'If'n there is the slightest chance of preventing carnage, then I have to take it,' he averred setting his hat straight. 'I'd never forgive myself if'n I didn't make the effort. The white flag should keep me safe. Even the most vengeful Indian will respect the peace totem.'

'But for how long?' muttered the sceptical wagon boss. 'At the first sign of betrayal, I'll have the boys ready to launch a blistering salvo in their direction. And it'll be Yellow Knife who we have in our sights.'

The two men shook hands. Just as Claymaker was about to step into the saddle for his fateful meeting, a low voice stayed his hand.

'Good luck to you, Mister Claymaker.'

He turned around. The speaker was clad in drab homespun garments befitting a woman on the trail.

Yet her face was smooth as satin unlike that of the average frontier wife. And the pair of large brown eyes that fastened on to his startled gaze were anything but mundane and ordinary. They shone brightly out of a stunningly beautiful countenance.

The woman offered him a winsome half smile. Flowing auburn tresses enfolded an oval face. The tough scouting veteran was lost for words. His whole frame trembled. Words formed on his lips, but failed to materialize. The two stared at one another for what seemed like a stack of moons. Nothing else mattered.

Finally a single word, hoarse and gravelly, leapt from the open maw.

'Lavinia??' He swallowed, immediately realizing that convention decreed a more formal greeting for two people on the cusp of a budding relationship. 'M-Miss Stapleton. Is-is it really you?' he stammered out. 'I . . . I. . . .'

'Go now, quickly,' the lady in question urged, not wishing to cause him embarrassment. 'You have important work to complete. I will still be here when you return. Then hopefully we can talk.'

The unexpected meeting had silenced the immigrant gathering. For a brief moment, their deadly ordeal was forgotten. All eyes were focussed on this astonishing tryst that had appeared out of the blue. The lady's urgent encouragement for her beau to resume his critical liaison with destiny broke the mesmeric spell.

Once again, their dangerous situation took precedence.

Jim Claymaker laid aside the untasted plate of food he had been handed. Then he scrambled on to his horse, forcing his thoughts back to the grim task ahead of him. The scrap of white cloth nailed to a stake was held above his head as he rode out into the open. A gentle trot some two hundred yards from the circle of wagons and he drew to a halt. There he waited. His heart was hammering louder than a Comanche war drum inside his chest.

Up on the ridge, the Indian chief and his commanders were muttering between themselves.

'It is Black Hair,' declared Broken Lance. 'He has escaped from the camp. I will shoot him down.' He raised a Springfield breech loader to his shoulder ready to despatch the fatal round.

'Hold fast, Broken Lance!' snapped the chief raising a hand 'He holds the sign of peace. We will ride down and talk.'

Slowly the deputation descended the slope halting some ten yards from the nervous scout. Yellow Knife was angry that the alleged killer of his son had escaped Comanche justice. But he was nevertheless intrigued to learn how it had been achieved. 'How did you escape from stake out, Black Hair?'

Claymaker shrugged off the question. He was more concerned about relaying the vital news concerning Running Bear. 'Your son is not dead, Yellow Knife. He recovered consciousness due to the ministrations of your medicineman. I counsel you to wait. Do not attack the wagon train.'

Broken Lance interrupted the scout's entreaty.

86

'Don't listen to the paleface dog. He lies. Black Hair only wishes to save his own skin and that of his murdering kind. Running Bear is dead. We all saw it for ourselves. There can be no mistake. And the Comanche want vengeance.'

Murmurs of agreement greeted Broken Lance's snarled indictment.

'What I say is true, great chief!' Claymaker exhorted. 'Do not heed the wild accusations of Broken Lance. All these people want is to cross your land in peace so they can settle further south in New Mexico. They do not seek trouble. Running Bear lives and he might be able to tell you what really happened out there when he was shot down. But it was not me, nor any of these people who carried out the foul deed.'

Some of the more virulent braves were siding with Broken Lance. Disbelief at the scout's protestation clouded angry faces that yearned for the glory of battle with the hated white eyes.

Only Yellow Knife was wavering. Could his son truly be alive?

That was when the tide inexorably turned.

EIGHT

. . . AND ATTACK!

A shot rang out from somewhere to the rear of the deputation of senior Comanches. It zipped past Claymaker's head. Blaize reared up on his hind legs. Suddenly all hell broke loose. Howls of dismay erupted from the mouths of the watching immigrants. The Indians were no less nonplussed at this sudden escalation of the tension.

Where had the shot come from? Haunted eyes flicked hither and thither, searching for the culprit.

Claymaker knew that the time for talking had passed. The shell had been fired in anger. Only one response could follow. He flung the white flag aside and swung round. This was no place to linger. A second bullet clipped the edge of his jacket.

'It's no use, boy. These varmints ain't for listening to reason.'

Bent low over the horse's neck he dashed back to

the wagon train. Luckily only five Indians had come down to parley. Those watching from the heights above the plain appeared to have been caught out by the surprise gunfire. He was thus able to launch Blaize into a flying leap just managing to clear one of the wagons. All the canvas covers had been removed to lessen the chance of fire spreading.

Even so, bullets skimmed by over his head. The arrows loosed from ash longbows were even closer.

Although Indians still purported to place their trust in spiritual protection, a pragmatic approach to battle ensured that they were always well armed. From an early age, the young brave was trained in the use of knife, tomahawk and the longbow. A proficient archer could rapidly loose a dozen accurately placed arrows to a distance of one hundred yards with supreme accuracy.

However, by the 1870s guns were becoming increasingly common amongst all the tribes. They were often decorated with tribal motifs and modified to suit individual preference. For long-distance fighting, they soon became more popular, much to the chagrin of the European pioneers. By the end of the plains wars, guns had replaced the ubiquitous longbow entirely.

Ruthless traders like Ira Gemmel were able to take full advantage of this new market. Somewhat removed from the main Indian force, Gemmel and his associate watched the proceedings from their hidden position. The two traders were concealed within a cluster of bushes set back so they could watch the action without becoming actively involved.

Gemmel scowled at his partner. 'You ought to have cut the skunk down,' he grumbled. 'Now he's managed to get back to the safety of the wagons.'

'I didn't have enough time to take aim,' protested Beedon jacking a fresh round into his Winchester carbine. 'That chief was thinking about turning tail. We had to stop him. You gotta admit it, Ira. Those two shots sure stirred up the pot. Now we have a full blown battle to enjoy. And with the whole Comanche nation buzzing around, those Concordia immigrants don't stand a chance.'

Gemmel nodded conceding his partner's assertion. 'Yeh, guess you're right there, Judas. And we have a splendid view from up here.'

The two conspirators watched open mouthed as the Indians began circling the wagons. Arrows thudded into the wagons while gunfire was exchanged by both sides as battle commenced. Initially the Indians kept to a safe distance as they assessed the strength of their enemy.

Claymaker had to borrow a couple of pistols, having been deprived of his own at the Comanche camp. They were an old army Remington chambered from the cap-and-ball loading, together with a .36 Navy Colt. The two separate calibres didn't help. But what the heck. At least he was now armed and ready.

The whereabouts of Miss Stapleton had to be thrust to the back of his mind. Survival of all the settlers was now his principal worry.

A howling yip of fury from the far side of the

parapet announced the first charge of the Indian forces. Yellow Knife proved himself to be no tenderfoot in the art of Indian warfare. His main force was held back in reserve. The initial bunch of warriors were ordered to make a frontal assault against the wagon defences at the point where Black Hair had re-entered the stockade.

The chief's objective was to test out the strength of their resistance.

There was a hurried dash as the men scrambled across to protect that side of the encampment. 'Some of you stay back,' Reed shouted out. 'This could be a ploy to draw our fire while the others attack from the rear.'

Both revolvers gripped firmly in his hands, Claymaker took up a position between two wagons. Nerves tight as bowstrings, there he waited behind a stout wooden dresser. 'Hold your fire, men!' he ordered. 'Don't shoot until I give the word. Choose a target, then let them have it.'

The defenders settled into their respective positions. The tension was palpable. Each man was cocooned in his own thoughts as the Comanche skirmishers thundered across the open sward. The scout could see that those men nearest to him were itching to let fly. 'Hold it! Keep your nerve, boys. Then we'll give them a surprise present they weren't expecting.'

It seemed that the charging attackers would overrun the barricade when the strident call came. 'OK, let's show these guys that we ain't no pushover! And make every shot count. Ready. . . . *Fire*!'

A deafening salvo of withering gunfire shook the ground. Smoke and hot lead from a myriad guns punched a hole in the charging phalanx. The scout had judged his timing to perfection. Half a dozen of the rampaging foe tumbled off their horses and lay still.

The survivors swerved away from the deadly fusillade firing their own weapons into the packed ranks of the defenders. Arrows from well aimed bows twanged as they thudded into the wooden emplacements. From the few sharp cries of pain, it was clear that some had found their mark. The gallant defenders had not had things all their own way.

As quickly as it had blown up, the attack had dissipated as the Indians returned to their positions on the surrounding ridges.

'You were right, Jim, when you said these red devils know how to make a guy sweat.' Fletcher Mason wiped a grubby bandanna across his brow. 'And this sure ain't from the big fella overhead.' He slung a thumb skywards pointing to the burning orb of fire. 'When do you figure they'll make their next move?'

'All part of the strategy,' replied Claymaker keeping a wary eye focused on the ridge top where the Comanche chieftain was poised. 'Yellow Knife knows that he has the upper hand. We ain't going no place. He can sit up there until our water runs out. Then pick us off much easier.'

Claymaker's brow furrowed in thought. 'My figuring is that he'll try a couple more forays and try to suss out our weak points. Then make a concerted attack there. Indians aren't the most patient of critters. They like to engage in battle rather than sit around laying down a siege. No kudos in that for young tearaways like Broken Lance. All they want is instant glory. And fighting is ultimately a young buck's prime means of attaining tribal status.'

'Here they come!' called out Pop Reed from further down the line. 'Make sure your weapons are fully loaded. Then give the varmints hell.'

A sonorous clicking of gun hammers and ratcheting of levers accompanied a deep sigh of nervous expectation. Every man, woman and child was ready for whatever the imminent affray would throw at them.

Over the previous few months on the trail, the settlers had toughened up. They had encountered small bands of Indians before. There had been a brief clash with a party of thieving Kiowa who had easily been driven off.

More persistent were the Osage raiders spurred on by hunger. They had dogged the train for a week making unsuccessful attempts to steal cattle. Pop Reed had judged it prudent to give the Indians three steers to avoid any bloodshed. It had satisfied the raiders who disappeared into the wilderness as quickly as they had materialized.

But this was the first major attack. Revenge rather than hunger drove the Indians this time. A fierce motivation that was far more perilous.

This second assault was far more circumspect. Yellow Knife had learnt from his previous foray that this band of white eyes was better prepared than he had expected. And that was down to the presence of Black Hair. His vehement curse on the lineage of the renowned army scout was tinged with respect. He was a worthy foe whom any Comanche chieftain would wish to confront. Completely forgotten now was the scout's claim that his son was still alive.

Yellow Knife's strategy proceeded as Jim Claymaker had suggested. His intention was to tease out any weak points. All too soon, bullets and arrows were raining down upon the defenders. Initially, there was a mighty adrenaline-fuelled response from the settlers. Fear and tension were released like air from a bursting balloon.

Smoke and the raucous din of battle quickly enveloped the ring of wagons.

Reed soon realized that by maintaining this rate of fire, they would all too soon run short of ammunition. Abandoning his post, he ran up and down behind the wagons relaying orders. Womenfolk were hard at work reloading guns while the older children handed them to fathers and uncles.

'Only fire when you have a target in your sights, boys. Don't waste bullets. That's what the critters want. Make every durned shot count.'

Arrows and lances twanged and thudded hard as they made contact with the wooden barricades. Bullets twined and ricocheted. Nobody was safe. Cries of anguish told of missiles that had found their marks. All too soon, spilled blood began to stain the yellow sand.

For some the dream of a new life on the frontier was cut short in brutal fashion.

Lives were tragically ended. Groans and screams issued from either side of the parapet indicating that both sides were suffering losses.

The Concordia lawyer was one of those to be struck down.

'Ugh!' he croaked as a bullet smashed into his arm. He reeled back clutching at the shattered appendage. One brave seeing the wounded man staggering into the open saw his chance to finish off his victim. The deadly foe urgently kneed his pony through a gap in the wagons where he dived headlong on to Fletcher's back. Both men tumbled to the ground.

'Aieeeeee!' crowed the leering red face. 'Revenge at last for Running Bear.' Whipping out a scalping knife, the brave grabbed a hold of the lawyer's thick main of black hair. The flashing blade rose to despatch the hated paleface invader. He had mistakenly taken the lawyer's copious tresses for those of Green River Jim.

Close by, the true owner witnessed the fatal attack. He had to move fast if Mason's life was to be saved. The Remington swung, the hammer dropping. But the old revolver chose that very moment to jam. Claymaker cursed. Only one thing for it. He flung the useless hunk of metal at the snarling Comanche.

His aim was instinctive and accurate. The Indian was knocked off balance as the weighty missile glanced off his head. The scout wasted no time. Snatching his own knife from the sheath affixed to his belt, he leapt at the sprawling assailant. The Indian was partially stunned though still dangerous. He saw the flashing knife blade in time to twist away. It sliced through his hide breeches burying itself in the sand.

First blood had been drawn. The two assailants drew apart facing one another.

A look of surprise at his error quickly merged into a lurid grin as the Indian's sneering visage recognized the famed army scout.

'So Black Hair, we meet again.' Broken Lance crouched down ready to attack. 'You will pay dearly for your treachery towards Yellow Knife.' He was also thinking of his own revenge against the man who had shamed him at Coal Creek. 'And this time there will be no escape. Prepare to die!'

The two adversaries met in a fierce life or death struggle. Razor-sharp blades clashed, the ring of metal discordant though well-defined above the fusillade of gunfire. Both were well versed in the deadly art of knife-wielding. Strength was the key as each man grasped his opponent's knife wrist.

Unfortunately Jim Claymaker's resilience was wilting. He had barely eaten a thing in three days. His ordeal in the Indian camp had not helped either. Muscles screamed in pain. Broken Lance sensed his opponent's weakened state. He was not slow in taking advantage of the scout's error of judgement. A handful of sand was scooped up and tossed into the white man's face.

The sleazy move brought a scream of triumph. 'Death to the white eyes!' screamed Broken Lance.

Claymaker staggered back trying to knuckle the stinging sand from his eyes. As Broken Lance lunged, intent on delivering the final *coup de grace*, a shot rang out. The single round was lost amidst the frenetic din of battle. Its impact, however, was devastating. The lead ball struck the rebellious Indian in the back, punching him forward. Blood poured from his open mouth. Clawing hands grasped the edge of a wagon before he slid to the ground and lay still.

Unaware of his miraculous deliverance from a sure and certain meeting with the grim reaper, Jim Claymaker floundered helplessly. It was only when a familiar voice penetrated the fog that he knew how close he had come to that terminal liaison.

Firm hands led him away. 'Are you all right, Mister Claymaker?' enquired the solicitous tones of Lavinia Stapleton. Gently she dabbed his eyes with water until the scout was able to focus on to his saviour. Was he in Heaven or Hell? A vision of loveliness amidst the devastation of mortal combat. Even though her face was smeared with grime, her hair dishevelled and awry, this woman was the most enchanting sight a man could wish to encounter.

'Was it y-you that s-saved me?' he stuttered while pouring a jugful of water down his parched throat. 'How can I ever th-thank you enough?'

'By doing what you know best, Mister Claymaker, and helping these people to reach Santa Rosa,' came back the firm but no less engaging reply.

The soothing words purred like a cat in his ears, although the loaded rifle in her hands spoke volumes.

Here was a woman not easily prone to alarmist panic-stricken reactions when danger came a-calling. A woman with whom he could settle down. Single-minded with a gritty determination, her declaration had reminded Green River Jim of the responsibilities he now shouldered.

He quickly shrugged off the recent encounter. The battle was still being waged all around. 'Plug that gap, boys,' he called out as a bunch of Indians made to penetrate the breach in their defences. Claymaker grabbed for his pistol suddenly realizing he was unarmed. The Navy Colt was empty and the Remington useless.

Miss Stapleton saw his dilemma and stepped in with a crisp response. 'Catch this, Jim,' she called out tossing over the Henry carbine she had just reloaded and used to deadly effect on Broken Lance.

'Much obliged . . . Lavinia.' A huge grin spread over his craggy features. The discomfiture of polite decorum had been gratefully surmounted. 'We have a lot to talk over.'

'But not now.' Her hauntingly mesmeric gaze swivelled towards the gap.

Claymaker swung and commenced firing alongside his colleagues. Hot lead soon disposed of the invaders.

A high-pitched whoop from the Comanche chief called his braves off. The raiders turned, galloping off out of range. Following this brief yet sustained assault on all points of the wagon circle, Yellow Knife needed to assess his casualties and method of attack. For the moment at least, there was a welcome lull in the fighting.

Bodies littered the battlefield. Yet they were far fewer than previously. The wider circle imposed following the initial skirmish had clearly benefitted the Comanche.

Behind the barricades, Pop Reed called a meeting to discuss their own way of dealing with the Indian problem. But first, the myriad wounds sustained in the attack required attention, some of it urgent. Luckily one of the immigrants was a doctor. He soon had the women organized into nursing duties.

One of the walking wounded who was soon dealt with was Fletcher Mason. His arm strapped up in a sling, he wandered across to join the conclave.

'Seems like I owe you my life, Jim,' he said. 'That redskin was all set to add my scalp to his belt.'

The scout couldn't contain a sardonic guffaw. 'And Miss Stapleton saved my bacon. Reckon we're all beholden to each other.'

'And that's how it should be,' piped up Pop Reed. 'Like the saying goes, all for one and one for all.'

'For a bunch of greenhorn settlers from Kansas, looks like we came out of that pretty well,' enthused Mason.

'We managed to keep 'em off this time,' Claymaker cautioned, his features reverting to a hard granite-like tenacity. 'But Yellow Knife is not about to give up. He has the manpower to wear us down. It'll soon be night. I figure that he'll throw a cordon around us then make a concerted attack at first light. Those guys are like a pack of wolves. They'll keep at us. His status as leader of the tribe is at stake. Not to mention revenge for believing I killed his son. And now his nephew has bitten the dust, he ain't about to smoke the pipe of peace.'

A sardonic eye flicked towards the crumpled form of Broken Lance. The stern resolve softened momentarily.

'All the same, you folks did well. Let's pray that we can hold them off.'

'If'n we're done with the mutual admiration, there's still a battle to be fought,' Reed interjected. 'Back to your posts, men. Here they come again.'

Enthused by his first major assault, Yellow Knife wasted no time in launching his final offensive of the day. A raucous bout of yipping and hallooing announced there arrival. Once again a ferocious battle for supremacy was engaged upon.

For the next hour, the Indian attack raged unceasingly. Casualties were registered on both sides of the barricades. Yet for every fallen Comanche, two were able to take his place. The settlers were not so fortunate. Their manpower was dwindling. The dead and wounded were slowly but steadily mounting up with no foreseeable chance of any replacements.

Claymaker was under no illusions that if the current situation continued, they would surely be overwhelmed. He shuddered to think what would happen if that was the outcome. The men would be killed, and not in a humane manner, the woman carried off to be sold as slaves. The best looking could expect to become the squaw of their captor. Just thinking of Lavinia in another man's tepee made Claymaker determined to find a solution to their dilemma.

A respite finally arrived with the onset of darkness. Fires were kindled and vittles prepared – while more wounded were tended. The bodies of the deceased were laid reverently to one side wrapped in canvas sheeting ready for burial.

Claymaker found a brief moment to converse with his betrothed in private. There was much to talk over. Neither could ever have envisioned that their budding partnership would be conducted under such trying circumstances. Nevertheless, the perilous situation in which they had unwittingly become embroiled had fashioned a degree of respect that both hoped would blossom into a more physical association.

Only time would tell. And the sandman was decidedly not on their team. The new day would bring forth another ferocious assault. Could they withstand much more of this incessant battering? Claymaker shook his head.

'Something bothering you, Jim?' murmured the woman's silky voice. 'Are you not ready to commit yourself to a woman who has made herself available through a mail order brochure?'

Claymaker was jerked from his morbid reflections. He quickly shook off the angst riddling his mind and took hold of the woman in his arms.

'Don't ever think that of me,' he gently chastized her. 'There is nobody in this world I would rather be with at this moment than you.' Their faces were inches apart. A kiss filled with passion was inevitable. Lavinia responded with all her heart and soul. It was a joyous moment for them both. Amidst the carnage of battle a brief moment of bliss shut out all the horror.

But it was one that could only ever be temporary.

The scout's thoughts were forced back to the present by a call from Pop Reed. With the greatest reluctance, like a pair of adolescent innocents, the love birds parted. Claymaker joined the conclave of immigrant elders to discuss their options while Lavinia helped the other women tend to the wounded and reload the guns.

A glum atmosphere pervaded the group of tired settlers. 'What are we going to do?' asked a morose Hank Smith of no one in particular. 'There's more than enough redskins out there to wear us down.'

Nobody had any realistic answer to the dilemma. Even Pop Reed was stymied. He had fought off Indians before. Most times they had only been scavenging after food or trying to steal horses. Small bunches that posed little threat. This was different. It looked like the whole Comanche nation had turned out to seek revenge for the killing of the chief's son.

'You gotten any ideas, Jim?' asked the wagon master.

There was only one way that any of them were going to come out of this dire predicament alive. And it was up to Green River Jim Claymaker to make it happen.

He voiced his thoughts as the new moon rose high into the night sky.

NINE

INTO THE DARK

Before answering Pop's tremulous query, Claymaker strolled across to the edge of the wagons. A half dozen pairs of anxious eyes followed him. There he paused staring out, trying to penetrate the blackness beyond. The moon had slid effortlessly behind a passing cloud. An orange glow indicated the spot where the Indians had made camp for the night in a cluster of cottonwoods. No doubt there were others encircling the marooned settlers with look-outs positioned at various points to keep an eagle eye on the wagon train.

The scout's rigid stance and furrowed brow indicated the myriad of possibilities racing around inside his head vying for dominance. Pipe dreams in the main with little chance of success. There was only one way to thwart Yellow Knife. Back straight, a resolute glint in his eye, Claymaker rejoined the gathering.

'If'n I could sneak through the Comanche lines, there's an even chance of reaching the army post at Fort Benson,' he declared in a level tone. 'A patrol of armed cavalry would shake the wind out of Yellow Knife's sails.'

'Reckon you could do it?' asked the gruff voice of Jake Sangster.

'If anyone can get through it's you, Jim,' concurred Pop Reed suddenly enthused with renewed hope. 'But it's one hell of a risk you'd be undertaking.'

'Could easily cost you your scalp,' added Fletcher Mason. 'Are you prepared to sacrifice your life for these people?'

The scout's whole body stiffened as he turned to face the group of expectant settlers. His face was set in a bleak yet determined mien. The reply was equally stoical and measured. 'Sure I could lose my hair. Yellow Knife has laid the blame for the killing of his son squarely on to my shoulders. And as I've tied in with you folks, he figures we're all equally guilty.'

'That slimeball Ira Gemmel has a heap to answer for,' railed the wagon master stamping his feet. 'If'n I ever get my hands on the lowdown rat he won't never make it to a court of law.'

A growl of accord greeted the fervent though somewhat impotent remark.

'That's why I have to make an attempt to bring help,' Claymaker stressed. 'It's the only way to bring

Yellow Knife to heel and stymie Gemmel's crazed notion to destroy this wagon train. You folks don't deserve to die out here in the wilderness. And it's up to me to do anything I can to ensure that you all reach Santa Rosa safely. I may not make it. But it won't be for want of trying.'

Lavinia Stapleton rushed across and threw herself into the brave scout's arms. She held him close in front of the whole gathering. Any awkwardness or embarrassment at such outwardly brazen behaviour was shrugged aside. Her man was laying his life on the line. She might never see him again. A romance that had been kindled and nurtured, suddenly threatened with extinction, was almost too much to bear.

Yet both of them knew that it had to be. There was no other way forward.

A passionate embrace, a melding of souls, and Jim Claymaker was ready to leave. With two freshly loaded Colt .45s donated by Jake Sangster, he quietly slid out between two wagons and disappeared into the stygian gloom of night.

The settlers muttered sombrely between themselves. Would they ever see the intrepid scout again? Such thoughts were at the forefront of every single one of the Concordia settlers. Particularly Lavinia Stapleton who was struggling to keep her tears at bay.

Emotional outbursts were considered unseemly in frontier communities. Resilience and tenacity were the essential attributes for coping with the many difficulties thrown in the path of immigrant settlers. Challenging and defeating the tough life facing these

106

pioneers demanded a hard exterior tempered with kindness and consideration for those in distress. They were God-fearing people who trusted in the Word evoked by the Good Book to see them through the hard times.

And so it was that following Jim Claymaker's departure, the Reverend Sylvan Dawkins led a prayer for the successful accomplishment of the hazardous undertaking. Never before had they despatched such a heartfelt and intense entreaty to their Maker. All they could do now was trust in the Good Lord's blessing.

Once the comforting presence of the wagon train had been cleared, Claymaker cat-footed across the open sward. Ever mindful of the lurking threat from watching eyes, he was soon forced to a halt. The opalescent ball overhead had chosen that precise moment to take an evening stroll. Sliding from behind a bank of cumulus, the landscape was illuminated by an ethereal silvery glow.

The slightest movement would be instantly spotted by an alert sentinel. The scout hugged the ground trying to make his body blend with the shadowy silhouettes all around. Many of them were the lifeless bodies of dead Indians. A macabre cemetery made all the more sinister by the presence of a paleface intruder.

Ten minutes passed. Claymaker's left leg was suffering from cramp. He yearned to stretch the aching limb. But any movement, however slight, could be his last. Gritted teeth and the knowledge that the lives of many people depended on his actions alone forced him to endure the jolting pain.

Thankfully, the moon decided to call time and once again slid back into obscurity. The scout heaved a sigh of relief as he stretched out the tight muscles. Concealed by the darkness, he crawled across the rest of the ground to the relative safety of a cluster of trees. Numerous campfires told him of the various Indian conclaves. What he needed to locate were their ponies.

Even though Jim Claymaker had been in many such situations as an army scout, his shredded nerves still jangled louder than a peel of church bells. Straining ears were constantly having to interpret the many and varied sounds: night creatures padding through the bushes, swaying branches and rustling leaves.

Avoiding the tell-tale Indian signs, he kept to the cover offered by the foliage. Food was being prepared on the open fires. The smell of roasting buffalo meat reminded him that his only sustenance in three days had been beef jerky and hard tack biscuits. It wasn't the first time he had gone without proper food. And it sure wouldn't be the last. Such was the life of a hunter and army scout.

Nevertheless, his stomach still rumbled. And to Claymaker it was loud enough to wake the dead. He forced his thoughts back to the task in hand. The odds were stacked against his successfully breaking out of the Indian cordon.

An optimistic attitude had always served him well

in the past. So maybe if'n he could get out of this predicament in one piece, he and Lavinia could make a new life for themselves. It was a big *if.* And he would have to call upon all his skills as a frontier scout to make it happen.

Thus far, he had not spotted any sign of guards. They must be there, skulking around in the under-growth. A measure of luck and his tracking ability had enabled him to avoid unwelcome contact.

He moved on. Continuing to push forward with feline grace through the sylvan shield, his acute hearing suddenly picked up an alien sound. Not the conspicuous prattle of Indians, these were voices with which he could more easily identify – the muted talk of white men.

It had to be Ira Gemmel and his weasel of a partner.

Perhaps if he drew closer, he could learn some-thing useful. The two men were stood on the edge of a low ridge on the far side of the basin that enclosed the wagon train. They were facing away from the stealthy watcher.

'Looks like two riders heading this way,' muttered Beedon.

'It's Sharky Mazola and Dutch Kramer,' added Gemmel in a surly tone. He was none too pleased to see his other lackeys. 'What do they want? I told them to keep away after they'd set that prairie fire going.'

The newcomers slid to a halt and dismounted.

'We heard all the shooting and came to investi-gate,' announced Kramer in a thick accent. 'Looks

109

like the whole Comanche nation is up in arms against that wagon train. And here are you guys with a grand-stand seat. What's the beef, Ira? We got stopped by a Comanche look-out down by the river.'

'Luckily he recognized us from when we sold him that firewater last month,' butted in Mazola. 'But we had to give him a free sample to allow us through.'

'That ought to keep the varmint happy for the night,' Judas Beedon chuckled.

Gemmel silenced his partner with an angry grunt. 'The fire you started in the Costilla Valley didn't work,' he snapped out. 'Those Concordia immigrants managed to get clear by crossing over the Canadian. They were helped by that interfering army scout called Green River Jim Claymaker.'

Kramer's eyes bulged. The scout's tough reputation was legendary.

'Don't worry, boys,' Beedon assured his sidekicks. 'He's stuck down there with the settlers. Ira's fixed things so that the Comanche will finish the job for us.'

'What's so darned special about this wagon train that it has to be wiped out to the last immigrant?' enquired Kramer uneasily 'Must be some hefty grudge you have with them, boss.'

Mazola nodded in agreement. Both men had been discussing Gemmel's top-heavy obsession. A couple of dudes taken down they could comprehend. But a whole wagon train? That was bordering on the unhinged. Had the boss lost his marbles? If so, the two underlings wanted no part of it. Especially when a guy like Jim Claymaker was involved.

Gemmel threw a look of warning towards his partner to curb his over-active tongue.

'That's no concern of your'n,' blustered Gemmel. 'I pay you good money to carry out orders, not to question them.' Then he tried to change the subject. 'Now quit your griping and let's get some grub. My belly's kicking up a fuss some'n awful. Those Indians have gotten more than enough for all of us to share in.'

The trader moved away without waiting for any reply. Mazola raised an eyebrow to his buddy and followed. It was true that they had lived well since joining up with Ira Gemmel. And the Indians sure appeared to have the upper hand in this fracas. So why rock the boat.

Once the treacherous bunch had left to assuage their hunger, Claymaker continued towards the outer cordon down by the river where the Indian ponies would be tethered. Now he knew for certain that Gemmel had arranged the range fire. Thus far, Lady Luck had guided his step. And those critters had provided advance warning of the Comanche sentinel. Hopefully he would have drunk himself into a stupor.

But like all females, the wily temptress had a habit of changing her mind at the most inopportune moment. That time had arrived. When he reached the river bank, the guard was nowhere to be seen. So far so good. It looked like his theory was correct. The firewater had done its job. And so it proved when he almost tripped over the supine body.

111

What he had not bargained for was a second guard who had wandered over to join his associate. Horses are a tribe's most important possession, hence the need for more than one guard.

As Claymaker led one of the horses away, the vigilant brave spotted the fleeting movement amongst the tree cover. He was almost in the clear when the Indian crept up behind him. Only the snickering of the pony sensing another presence alerted him to the danger.

The Comanche darted in for the kill. His knife rose to despatch the army scout into the hereafter. Claymaker swung round to meet the attack, twisting to one side as the deadly blade whistled past his head. A heavy-weight punch that thudded into the Indian's stomach elicited a whoosh of pain. The knife spun away into the darkness.

Claymaker wasted no further time in tackling the brave. The cat was now out of the bag and he needed to get clear before he was overwhelmed.

The Indian quickly recovered his wits and let out the strident warning call of a bald eagle. The universal warning sign of danger was followed by a vocal summons to arms. 'Black Hair has tricked us! He has escaped from the wagon train.' The Indian sentinel was now on his feet. 'Up my brothers or he will bring help from the blue coats.'

In a trice the air was filled with the clamour of moccasined feet. In amongst them was the thud of leather boots. Food was forgotten. Gemmel and his men were more concerned to prevent Claymaker reaching the nearest army post at Fort Benson than filling their bellies.

The moon also decided to join the action by showing his face one again.

'There he goes,' Beedon shrieked. 'Get after him, boys. Don't let the varmint escape. If'n he reaches the fort we're done for.'

The scout leapt on to the back of the pony. Snatching up the bridle he mercilessly lashed the switch across the animal's flanks urging it to a full gallop. Bare-back riding is a skill that few white men had mastered. Even the Indians often used light saddles of buffalo hair.

The animal Claymaker had selected was ready bridled but had no saddle or blanket. He was forced to control it with his knees, balance being the key to staying on the animal's back. It was a tiring practice but one that the scout had perfected. His only problem now was to outride his pursuers.

But this little Indian pony was no flyer. What he wouldn't give at that moment to be on the back of his beloved appaloosa, Blaize. No point regretting what can't be changed. He urged the cayuse onward across the rolling terrain.

The pace was too hot for the horse which soon began to tire. The Indians along with Gemmel and his gang were catching up. His only hope was to reach the deep ravine ahead. Rio Concho was a tributary of the Canadian. At the place to which Claymaker was heading it passed through a steep-sided gorge. Only the most foolhardy, or desperate

113

rider would challenge the dangerous rapids that thrashed and cavorted through the compacted narrows.

As far as Jim Claymaker was concerned, he had been given no choice in the matter.

TEN

A WATERY GRAVE?

The fleeing scout urged the mustang to its limits as he drew close to the lip of the vertical cliff face. The wild-eyed animal seemed to recognize the extreme peril into which it was about to plunge. All the rider's strength and skill was required to control the terrified beast.

'Come on you mangy critter,' he hollered out with gusto, digging his heels in. Forced onwards, the horse was given no option but to plough onward into the unknown, its nostrils flared in manic abandon, eyes wide and imploring. Claymaker ignored the plea for mercy. All his pent-up energy was fully absorbed in the crazy endeavour. Mouth open wide, he vented his exhilaration in one almighty howl of delight.

'Yeeeeehaaaaagh!!'

It was the only way he could have contemplated such a suicidal escape from certain capture by his pursuers. The slightest hesitation on his part and he would have been doomed. Maybe even now, he was heading for an early and extremely watery grave. But there was little time to consider such a macabre outcome.

Suddenly without any warning he was air-born.

The cold night air whipped past snatching the plainsman from his head and catching his long hair. The manic scream echoed back from the stark walls of the ravine slapping Claymaker in the face. For what seemed like a handful of eternities, the pair of flyers drifted through the dark sky. Was this how a diving buzzard felt as it homed in on its prey?

The moon's iridescent glow was reflected off the thrashing waters below. Any moment now and they would hit the surface. And then what? Total oblivion? Such thoughts flashed momentarily through the scout's churned up brain.

'Here we gooooo!' he shouted at the snorting cayuse. Both man and beast stiffened automatically as the imminent crash drew near.

Claymaker launched himself off the mustang's back. They hit the water separately, both disappearing below the turbulent surface. Thankfully at this point, the gorge was deep enough to prevent serious injury. The impact almost knocked the man unconscious, although the icy water soon brought him round. Floundering helplessly, he immediately struck out for the surface. The snorting cayuse was close by. It

116

appeared unhurt.

Gratitude at thwarting the Grim Reaper's attempt to gain a new recruit brought a gasp of relief. The scout's next thought was to glance up at the rim of the cliff from which he had so recently jumped.

The pursuers had reached the overhang. Much to his chagrin, they had spotted him. Puffs of smoke from rifles were quickly followed by spouts of water where the bullets struck the surface. The roar of gunfire filled the gorge. It would not take them long to zero in on his wallowing situation. Something had to be done if he was to survive.

There was only one thing for it.

He released a chilling howl of anguish.

'Aaaaaaagh! I'm hit!'

Arms flailing in a wildly exaggerated manner, he sank beneath the churning surface. The avowed intention was to fool the critters into thinking they had struck lucky.

It appeared to be a successful ploy. Up on the rim, Ira Gemmel also emitted a yell. But his was of triumph. 'Yikes, boys, we got the bastard!'

'No need to worry about that interfering busybody anymore,' sang out an exultant Judas Beedon. 'With Claymaker out of the picture, we're in the clear.'

'Running Bear has been avenged,' declared one of the accompanying Indians. 'Now we can return to finish off the paleface invaders.'

'You fellas get back to join Yellow Knife,' Gemmel said to them. 'We'll stick around for a spell just to make sure Black Hair don't rise from his watery grave.'

The group of Comanche braves swung around and headed back to rejoin their comrades, leaving the searching eyes of Gemmel and his men to scan the angry turmoil of the Rio Concho. They could see the Indian pony struggling out of the fermenting eddy on the far shoreline. But of Jim Claymaker there was no sign.

'Sure looks like that troublemaker has cashed in his chips all right,' averred Dutch Kramer moving across to his horse.

But Gemmel was more cautious. 'That skunk has more lives than a bob cat,' he snorted. 'We'll hang around a spell longer to make certain he don't suddenly return from the dead. Keep your eyes peeled, boys. Anything moves, give it some lead.'

They remained on the lip of the ravine for another ten minutes. Gemmel was taking no chances. Too often in the past, the army scout had defeated the odds against him. As a result he had no intention of being fooled again. Had they known the truth, the braggarts would have had the smirks wiped from their kissers.

Lungs bursting, blood pounding inside his head, Jim Claymaker had used all nine of his cat lives in that last few minutes. He finally surfaced from the thrashing rapids in a clump of reeds. Close by, the pony was nibbling on some grass as if nothing untoward had occurred. A glance up to the cliff edge told the wily scout that Gemmel was still keeping a close watch.

He had to remain perfectly still while the bad guys were up there. But a freezing body was making him shiver. By now the first traces of dawn were breaking over eastern horizon. Although the ravine was in shadow, there was enough light for the gang to spot any movement down below, any shift of position.

'Sure looks like he ain't gonna be troubling us no more,' remarked Beedon rubbing his hands with satisfaction. The others avidly agreed. That was one slippery customer they were more than glad to be rid of.

Ira Gemmel was also satisfied that Green River Jim Claymaker had returned to the element that had given him his nickname.

'OK, boys, let's get back to the show. I want the best seat in the house to see those damned settlers meet a fitting end.' The light of the false dawn revealed a malicious gleam in the devious trader's eyes as he mounted up. 'And I'm gonna enjoy every second watching the action.'

The others threw him a look of puzzlement. They still had been given no inkling as to their boss's motives. And Gemmel did not react well to being interrogated. Dutch Kramer knew that it was the wise man who kept his own counsel. No doubt all would be revealed in due course. At least that snooping army scout had been effectively dealt with.

Once the buzzards had left, Claymaker hauled himself out of the river. He stripped off his wet duds squeezing out the water. His teeth were chattering twenty to the dozen. Reeling drunkenly away from the water's edge, he sought out some desiccated grass in which he rolled to dry his chilled body.

There followed what seemed like the performance of a dancing flea. At least the vigorous exercise managed to instil some much-needed warmth into the lean torso. But no more time could be lost if'n he was to reach Fort Benson in time. Naked as the day he was born save for his boots, the scout mounted up. The wet buckskins were laid across the horse's shoulders. They would quickly dry once the sun rose above the serrated rim of the gorge.

Luckily he still had both his revolvers. They would also need drying out.

Downstream an ever increasing tumult looked like it was heading for a waterfall. So his only hope was to follow the river back to where it was shallow and calm. An hour later he located a safe place to cross. The sun was now well up. Its warmth was a blessing to be fully appreciated following that soaking in the Rio Concho.

From there he headed north west. By keeping the sun behind and little to the left he was able to maintain a steady canter across the white expanse of alkali salt flats towards the distant upthrust of the Sangre de Cristos Mountains. Fort Benson lay beyond in the Saguache Valley.

He resisted the temptation to push the mustang harder. But curbing his impatience was a strain on the nerves. A regular if irksome plod was the only way to reach the army outpost. At his current rate he would not be there before noon of the following day at the earliest.

Frustration ate at the scout's normally mellow temperament.

Then, as the sun reached its zenith, he noticed a plume of dust in the distance. Caution made him draw rein and pause behind some boulders. As the dust cloud grew in strength, a column of riders took shape.

'An army patrol,' the scout blurted out. 'And heading this way. That sure is a lucky break.'

Claymaker nudged his pony out on to the trail and waited for the troop of cavalry to arrive. He did not have long to wait.

'Morning, lieutenant,' he greeted the young officer leading the patrol. 'Am I glad to have met up with you guys.'

The officer saluted, instantly recognizing the famed army scout. His startled look indicated that he was surprised to encounter the scout in such a remote place. 'Jim Claymaker!' he exclaimed. 'What in thunder are you doing out here?'

The scout answered the officer's query by quickly outlining his recent adventures with the wagon train and the death of the Indian chief's son.

'Yellow Knife is on the warpath, Lieutenant.' Mention of the Comanche chieftain and the urgency in Claymaker's request saw all the troopers crowding round to listen in. 'Those settlers need help, and quickly if'n they're gonna survive.'

'How many Indians are there?' interjected Lieutenant Josh Hardacre.

'Looked to me like the whole darned Comanche nation has turned out,' came back the earnest reply. 'On this old hoss it'll take me until doomsday to reach the fort. If'n you ride like the devil, you could get there in double-quick time. Fresh mounts and a full contingent of troopers is the only way those poor folks can be saved.'

The young officer recognized the pressing need for action. He immediately issued orders for a return to Fort Benson.

'We're abandoning our hunt for Broken Lance, sergeant,' the officer called out. 'This is far more important. Have the men about turn ready for a hard ride back to the fort.'

'Much obliged, lieutenant,' effused the grateful scout. 'I'll back track and try to locate the skunks that started all this. You should know that Broken Lance was killed in the attack on the wagon train. He tried lifting my hair. But I was lucky that someone else was on hand to shoot him down before the knife slipped.'

Explaining the part played by Lavinia Stapleton in the grim incident was passed over. A man had to uphold his reputation as a tough frontiersman at all costs to be taken seriously by the military.

Hardacre smiled. 'Saves us a job at least.'

The small patrol was soon heading back at a fast clip in the direction of Fort Benson. Within minutes they had disappeared in a cloud of dust. Claymaker gave thanks that he had encountered them. Now he could get back and keep tabs on Gemmel and his cohorts. The element of surprise was in his favour since they figured he was in the Reaper's clutches.

ELEVEN

GEMMEL SHOWS HIS HAND

It was a much slower journey back to the Canadian River for Jim Claymaker. His temper was becoming ever more volatile on account of the mustang's flagging stamina. For the last few miles the poor critter stumbled wearily almost throwing its rider. The scout had been forced on numerous occasions to dismount and rest the animal. But he could not afford to be cast afoot, so managed to curb his exasperation.

Finally he spotted the line of trees adorning the ridge overlooking the river valley. He urged the blowing horse up the last steep grade. But it was no use. The animal was done in. It stumbled and fell to the ground.

Claymaker cursed aloud before conceding that the small horse had done its best, given its all. A murmur akin to an apology for his forceful goading rumbled in his throat. Normally he displayed respect for his four-legged associates. But his current predicament was anything but routine.

The horse needed despatching. A bullet was out of the question. It could easily alert the villains. 'Sorry about this, old gal,' he muttered sliding the bowie knife from its belt sheath. 'But it's the best I can manage.'

A swift slash across the mustang's throat elicited a choking gurgle as blood gushed from the fatal wound. He stood back as flecks of scarlet splashed his boots. But this was no time for dawdling.

On reaching the ridge a half hour later, caution demanded a halt on the edge of the trees. Gunfire together with the clamorous swell of hollering from the redskins indicated that the battle was still raging. At least it proved that the settlers were holding out. Great care was needed as he pushed through the shrubbery.

He was well aware that Gemmel and his crew would be somewhere close by, observing the desperate life-and-death struggle. Doubtless they were urging the Comanche assailants on to finish the job quickly. The scout cursed under his breath. These rats were like odious vultures waiting to pick over the human remnants. Nausea at the thought of such vile depredation made the scout's stomach lurch.

A couple of burned out wagons had been removed from the circle. Their blackened husks were like the bones of a stricken animal picked clean by scavengers.

More sombre were the line of wooden crosses where dead immigrants had been buried during a lull in the fighting. Claymaker swallowed, the lump in his throat brought tears to his eyes. Was one of the crosses for Lavinia? No sense in dwelling on such a sombre notion. He needed to remain positive.

From his position, it was impossible to tell how many survivors there were. Ammunition must surely be running low. With any luck, the cavalry should be here soon. They had to be moving considerably faster than he had managed. There was no way that he could join up with the settlers and raise their spirits with news that a rescue was imminent. And being cast a foot did not help.

The scout's features hardened as he thought of the varmint responsible for his and the settler's plight. Whatever reasoning the rat's warped brain had manufactured, nothing could explain away the pain and suffering he had inflicted on these innocent travellers. His eyes scanned the terrain seeking to pinpoint the odious sidewinder.

'When I catch up with you, mister,' he muttered under his breath, 'the rule book won't count for nothing.'

He pushed through the undergrowth. Silence was essential if'n he was to get close to the skunks. Some time later, with the din of battle raging in his ears, he caught the sound of voices coming from the far side of some rocks. Peering round the edge, his eyes widened. Then a slow smile broke out on the craggy façade.

It was Gemmel and his three sidekicks. And all their attention was focussed on the battle down below. Nodding heads told that they were satisfied with the way things were going. Gemmel signalled his intention that a break was called for.

The four brigands then moved away from where the action was taking place and wended their way downhill to a shaded hollow where a camp had been set up. Bedrolls were laid out around the embers of a smouldering fire.

They were about to get the shock of their miserable lives when he upset their plans. Tentatively so as not to disturb any stones, the scout snook up as close as he dared. The men were pouring coffee from a blackened pot bubbling over the fire.

Gemmel was clearly in a good mood. He poured a liberal slug of whiskey into each of their mugs.

'Here's a toast to a job well done,' he boasted lifting his mug. The others echoed his jubilation. They obviously expected Yellow Knife to finish the job soon. Claymaker was seething. But what he heard next brought a gasp of surprise that almost revealed his illicit presence.

'Those critters can't hold out much longer, Judas,' Gemmel remarked to his partner. 'It'll soon be over. Then I can rest easy. One or two settlers could have been handled. But when those Concordia dupes upped sticks and headed this way, I needed to take drastic steps.'

'When are you gonna fill us in on what these people have done that's ruffled your feathers so much?' asked Beedon.

'Yeh, boss. What gives?' seconded Dutch Kramer. 'Me and Sharkey have a right to know seeing as we're laying our lives on the line.'

Gemmel was feeling effusive. 'Guess you have at that, boys,' he obliged magnanimously. 'There ain't no harm in telling you now. We're all in this together now. Sink or swim.'

He laid a beady eye on his underlings, silently challenging them to make an issue of his implied threat.

Kramer and his buddy remained tight-lipped. So Gemmel offered them both a cigar to lighten the tension.

'It's like this,' he began. 'Back in '65, the War was over and there was money to be made by those willing to lend their skills to it.' He smirked at the staring faces. 'Mine were in these.' He raised his hands. 'Shuffling pasteboards around the green baize was a sight more profitable than hard labour in the fields. And for a while I did perty damn good.'

Then things began to go awry.

On this particular occasion, he had lost all his money in a high stakes poker game in Abilene. Forced to leave town in a hurry when he couldn't honour his IOUs, Gemmel had fled north. All he had left were the clothes on his back and a horse. He had, however, been astute enough to keep a lifeline in the First National Bank for just such an occurrence. It wasn't much, just enough to give him a grubstake in a new town.

Plodding across the endless sea of waving grass, he

had nothing much to occupy his thoughts save the sorry position in which he now found himself.

His brow furrowed. The morose gambler was certain he had been cheated by that conniving house dealer operating from the Prairie Dog Saloon. Yet much as he tried, he failed to suss out how the twist had been made. Gemmel thought he was party to all the tricks these tinhorns pulled. But this was a new scam that had cleaned him out.

Two days later he rode into the town of Concordia some twenty miles to the north west. It was a sleepy berg in which not much seemed to be happening. Just another hick prairie town catering to the needs of homesteaders. A jumping off point for those heading west.

The latest batch of Conestoga wagons was being assembled on the edge of the settlement. Surely but steadily, the new frontier was spreading westwards. That was where the future lay. But not on a farm. The back-braking toil of the sodbuster was not Ira Gemmel's idea of the new utopia. His intention of achieving the good life was through far more profitable means.

His dream was to build up a trading empire based in one of the new breed of towns opening up in the south west. Buy goods cheaply from Mexico and sell them at a handsome profit to the immigrants. A smart dude like him could easily eliminate any competition with the help of a few hard-boiled toughs to back his play.

Money and plenty of it was the key to success in

such an enterprise. But how was he going to make enough to fulfil his dream?

Then an idea struck him. An article in the local newspaper in Abilene had hinted that the railroad was being extended further west. Land on either side of the proposed track line was for sale. Those with the funds to buy a plot could make a huge profit when the Kansas Pacific Company's land buyers arrived. The never-ending unsettled prairie grasslands to the west were open terrain for anyone to settle.

A plan quickly formed in the devious mind of the failed gambler. If'n he could persuade folks that the next stop on the railroad was to be Concordia, perhaps that was how he could make his poke. After all, the town was not that far north of the current route. Then, once he'd amassed enough dough, he could disappear before the gullible mugs were any the wiser.

His slush fund would provide the necessary back-up. Luckily, the First National had a branch in town. Once he was set up in business, all he had to do was haul in the punters and collect their dough.

A fancy printed deed of ownership from his so-called Eldorado Land Agency would seal the contract making it appear genuine. It sounded good. Already, after just a few minutes intense thought and speculation, he was rubbing his hands with glee at the money to be made.

'You ain't just a handsome face,' he murmured to himself. 'There's a sharp brain inside here.' He tapped his head. 'Pity you didn't use it before.'

The only fly in the ointment was if anybody came north who knew the true course of the railroad. But that was only a slight risk if'n he moved fast. Communications were slow in this direction. Everybody was heading due west. The new cattle trails stopped at the rail head to the south. Nobody was looking north west. The cunning fraudster's eyes panned across the spread of the town. A sly grin creased his rubicund features. No telegraph wires. This berg really was isolated.

He would need a partner though. And who better to reel in the suckers than his younger brother, Cyrus. The guy would be just as eager to acquire some easy money as his older kin. Last he heard, the boy was holed up in Leavenworth working for a freight-hauler. He would be more than eager to ditch that.

After booking a room at the only hotel in town, the Silk Purse, he wrote a letter to Cyrus outlining his plan and mailed it off. With any luck the kid should be here within a week. If'n his innate charm with the dames was anything to go by, Cyrus would have no dif-ficulty guiding gullible patrons into the spider's web.

Then he went in search of a suitable office from which to conduct his business transactions. Within the hour a single room shack was rented. And within two days, the Concordia branch of the nationally acclaimed Eldorado Land Agency was up and running. A smart suit and second hand office furni-ture cleaned him out. But it was going to be worth every last cent.

For the next few days until his brother arrived,

Gemmel senior was forced to pay for his meals on tick. The suit and his spectacles gave him an air of respectability which persuaded local traders that his credit was sound.

Each day, he waited near the stage coach depot hoping to see Cyrus step down. It was on the fifth day that the younger Gemmel alighted with his carpet bag.

'Am I glad to see you, brother,' Ira declared expressing his relief by slapping the boy on the back. 'I'm down to my last silver dollar. Never thought I'd be in such dire straits. But it's all about to change now that you're here.'

'What's this all about?' posited the puzzled young man. 'Your letter hinted that big bucks were just waiting to be scooped up in this berg.' He looked around sniffing the air sceptically. 'Don't seem much of a place to me.'

Nobody could ever have mistaken them for brothers. Cyrus was taller and much leaner than his older kin. Where Ira had allowed his penchant for booze and good food to take control, Cyrus had kept himself in good shape. Hence his success with the ladies who doted on his irresistible magnetism.

And that was what Gemmel intended making use of. The kid's gift of the gab would persuade clients that investing in Eldorado land holdings was a sure-fire way to a quick profit.

'That's cos you ain't got the imagination, little brother,' Gemmel chided genially. 'When I tell you what I have in mind, you'll soon change your tune.'

131

They wandered over to the Palace Bar where Ira explained in detail how they were going to fleece the good citizens of Concordia. His last silver dollar paid for the drinks. 'But it all depends on you persuading folks they're on to a good deal.'

'And how do I do that?'

'By hinting that you have it on good authority that the Kansas Pacific have decided at the last minute to take a more northerly route across the plains. And it will be passing through Concordia. Anybody holding land in this area will see their investment double or treble in value overnight. That should wet their appetites.'

'Ain't they gonna get suspicious when no company reps come to suss out the terrain?'

'By then, we'll have their cash in our hands and made a swift exit well before the penny drops.' Gemmel was gushing with enthusiasm for his nefarious scheme. 'Nobody will figure they've all been hoodwinked until it's too late. By then, we'll have disappeared into the wide blue yonder.'

'I like it,' Cyrus concurred raising his glass in a toast. A grin as wide as the Mississippi spread across his handsome features. 'Never figured you for such a devious character.'

'We have to use what the Good Lord gave us if'n we're to make our mark in life,' effused the cocky braggart nonchalantly imbibing a slug of whiskey. 'And in my case that has to be a fertile brain. And it's a darned sight better than risking life and limb holding up banks and stagecoaches.'

'More profitable too,' added his brother with a nod. 'If'n this caper succeeds, we'll soon be living on easy street.'

Cyrus played his part to perfection. Subtle hints were spread throughout the town that the railroad extension was heading for Corncordia. Anyone who invested in land adjacent to the proposed route was sure to make a handsome return on their investment. And how was this land to be obtained? Why two blocks down the street at the newly opened office of the Eldorado Land Agency, of course. There was a map pinned on the wall with all the plots being sold off.

'I'm heading down that way myself right now to get a piece of the action,' declared the cocky young fox raising his derby with a flourish. 'If'n you folks are as smart as I figure, you'll do the same. That lands gonna be snapped up like Scotch whiskey.'

And with that incisive comment, he hurried off to spread the word elsewhere.

As anticipated, there was a rush to obtain the necessary deeds of covenant. Money changed hands and there were smiles of anticipation all round. Within days the dough was flowing into the pockets of the two charlatans. It appeared that they had found the goose that lays the golden eggs. With a rapidity that shocked even the quick silver Ira Gemmel, the number of available lots on the map diminished.

As with all such tricksters, however, the grasping tentacles of avarice proved their undoing. The wise gambler knows when to call time and cash in his chips. Ira assumed that the influx of dough would continue unabated until all the alleged plots of land had been sold.

Accordingly, he stayed in Concordia longer than was prudent.

And the inevitable happened on the fifth day.

A representative of the Kansas Pacific Railroad was passing through on his way to check on the extension of the line beyond Abilene. What he learned while taking a drink in the Palace Bar was nothing short of mind-boggling. The cat was out of the bag. The town marshal was summoned and a deputation of irate citizens immediately descended on the Eldorado office.

Bursting through the door, the two fraudsters were caught in the act of duping yet another credulous sap.

'The game's up, you pair of phonies,' snapped the lawman drawing his Remington .44. 'There ain't no railroad coming to Concordia. Mister Fargo here has scuppered your scam good and proper. Now hands up. You rats are heading for the hoosegow.'

Ira was stunned into submission. His hands rose. But not so his brother.

'Nobody's taking me in,' Cyrus snarled, slapping leather.

His gun was half out of the holster when a dozen bullets took him down. Even when it was clear he was dead, hot lead continued thudding into the body until the lawman called a halt. Cyrus Gemmel looked like a red colander. It was not a pretty sight. Ira could only stand and stare, open mouthed.

In the space of a minute, his grandiose plan had disintegrated, and his only kin was a bloody mess on the floor.

The trial was a foregone conclusion. The charlatan was given six years hard labour in the Kansas state penitentiary at Fort Leavenworth.

But ever the resourceful operator, he managed to escape with an associate after only a year behind bars. The two sidekicks went into the business of robbing stagecoaches. In this they proved to be a highly successful pair of road agents. That is until one heist went badly wrong. Gemmel managed to escape but his partner was killed.

That was the writing on the wall. He had enough money stashed away to head west where he was able to establish a thriving general store in the New Mexico town of Santa Rosa. That was until he learned that the town of Corcordia had been burnt to the ground in a lethal prairie fire.

Now, many of the citizens who had lost dough due his conniving sting were heading his way. And others were bound to follow if'n their friends sent back positive reports.

TWELVE

MORE STARTLING NEWS

'That's why they have to be stopped,' the angry trader emphasized, punching a fist into the palm of his hand. 'Not only did they cause me to spend a miserable year in the pen, they murdered my brother. And for that they're gonna pay the full penalty. Ira Gemmel ain't going back to Leavenworth for anyone.'

Nobody had the nerve to disabuse him of the fact that it was all of his own doing.

It was indeed a surprising revelation. And not only for Gemmel's associates. Jim Claymaker was equally stunned at the grim tidings so recently overheard. It explained everything. The fraudulent trader was scared of being eyeballed by those members of the wagon train who knew him and had lost all their

136

savings due to his unscrupulous chicanery.

That meant the whole lot had to be eradicated.

'Well it looks like your wish is going to be granted, Ira,' remarked Judas Beedon. 'Yellow Knife looked like he was about to launch his final charge. There's no way the survivors can hold out much longer against these constant attacks. By sundown your prayers will be answered and they'll be history. Then we can pick up in Santa Rosa where we left off.'

Gemmel grinned widely. 'Everything is turning out just like I planned after all.'

But the gang were in for a shock. And it arrived in the daunting figure of Big Bull, the tribal medicine-man. The gang had been so enthralled by Gemmel's disclosure, they had failed to heed his arrival. The shaman wrestled his mount to a juddering halt beside the white men.

Grim expressions of unease clouded the four faces.

'Why in the name of blue blazes are you in such an all-fired hurry?' Gemmel snapped at the panting soothsayer.

Big Bull could hardly get his staggering news out fast enough. 'Running Bear is alive! I, Big Bull – greatest of all the Comanche medicinemen – have delivered our noble chief's son out of the darkness.'

Gasps of speechless amazement greeted this impossible revelation. Gemmel was the first to recover his wits. 'That can't be true. He was dead. I saw it with my own eyes. Ain't that the goddamned truth, Judas?'

'Sure is,' agreed his partner. 'He can't have survived. The kid was dead all right.'

Big Bull was undeterred by the disbelief of the white traders. He was well used to protestation from those unfamiliar with what he felt were legendary powers granted by a high authority from the spirit world. 'It is as I say. Running Bear has been brought back from the great beyond. It is the will of Manitou, the great spirit. He is weak and cannot be moved. But the boy will recover.'

'You certain about this, Big Bull?'

Gemmel was playing for time. This was the last thing he needed. When Yellow Knife realized that his son was indeed still alive, his need for revenge would disappear like the desert wind. It mattered little that settlers were crossing Comanche land now. The two factions could easily reach an amicable agreement in that respect.

The medicine-man was becoming impatient. 'You dare to say that Big Bull lies? What I say is truth.' His hand gripped the lance he was toting a little tighter. 'Now tell me where Yellow Knife is? The chief's heart will leap with joy when he hears of this momentous happening.'

Gemmel pointed to the ridge. 'He's over the far side of the rim. Reach the top and you'll have a grandstand view of the action.'

Without another word being spoken, Big Bull swung his horse in the direction indicated. Gemmel's face remained unmoved as he drew his pistol and aimed it with deliberate ease at the back of the unsuspecting medicineman. The bullet struck him dead centre. An apt description of the result. The tribal soothsayer threw up his arms and tumbled from his horse.

The ceremonial headdress fell to one side revealing nought but a withered, dried up old prune. All of the soothsayer's charisma disappeared along with his life.

'Seems like old Big Bull is human after all, and heading for the Happy Hunting Grounds a mite before he expected.' The killer's menacing guffaw was heralded by the others.

'Best place for him,' echoed Judas Beedon. 'The last thing we need is for Yellow Knife to back off now he's almost finished those suckers off.'

Gemmel tossed the dregs of his coffee mug on to the fire. 'OK boys, reckon it's about time we checked on how the final showdown is going. Then we need to head back to the Indian encampment to stop Running Bear spilling what he knows. Let that happen and we're all done for. If'n the Comanche don't get us, the army sure will.' He kicked sand over the embers of the fire. 'I don't know about you guys, but Ira Gemmel sure ain't ready to be measured for a wooden overcoat yet awhile.'

Once again, Jim Claymaker was shocked by what he had just heard and witnessed. But ever the consummate professional, he quickly recovered his wits. He had the edge here. The element of surprise would outweigh the odds of one against four. Gun in hand, he jumped into the open challenging the four brigands to surrender.

'First critter that reaches for his hogleg is dead

meat,' came the blunt command. The gang had been caught on the hop. Claymaker wasted no time in superfluous interchange. 'Now unhook those gun-belts real slow and toss them aside.' The threatening pistol wagged ominously. 'After what you skunks have pulled, my trigger finger is getting mighty nervous.'

'Claymaker!' Beedon's shocked expletive had frozen him to the spot. 'Where in thunderation did you spring from?'

Gemmel was less than eager to comply. Capitulation now was a one-way ticket to meet the hangman. Dutch Kramer was nonplussed at the sudden change of fortune. He was slightly forward and to the right of the gang boss. Gemmel saw his chance and took it. He lunged at the hardcase and pushed him firmly towards the scout. Kramer floundered as he tumbled forward spoiling Claymaker's aim.

Within seconds all hell broke loose. Sensing this was the only opportunity they were going to get, the others slapped leather. Smoke billowed from gun barrels as bullets hissed through the air. Claymaker was forced on to the back foot. Bullets were flying every which way. He snapped off a couple of wild shots as he retreated to the safety of some nearby rocks. The first struck Kramer at almost point blank range. The Dutchman screamed and went down clutching his shoulder.

Slugs plucked at the scout's buckskins. Others whined off nearby rocks.

Gemmel had also backed off in the opposite direc-tion. His gun bucked in his fist. Beedon was stuck in the middle, caught in a crossfire. His hat disappeared. Another bullet singed his right hand forcing him to release the pistol. He fell to the ground writhing to one side desperately seeking shelter. But there was none to be had. It looked like he was a certain goner.

Sharkey Mazola was kneeling down returning Claymaker's fire when a bullet struck him in the leg. That was when another sound cut through the hammer of small arms fire. A bugler's call to arms came from behind announcing the arrival of the cavalry. Momentarily there was a lull in the action as all eyes swung towards the source of the strident directive.

The sight of cavalry troopers in blue uniforms, swords drawn and bearing down on them, was too much for the remaining braggarts. Sharkey Mazola threw down his gun and raised his hands. Beedon was no hero and quickly joined him. Kramer was still groaning on the ground. Smoke drifting across the site of the short-lived gunfight soon dispersed showing the solid figure of Green River Jim covering them from behind a boulder.

'Don't anybody move,' he bellowed above the din of pounding hoofs.

The troop led by Colonel Sourby hustled to a halt. It was a testament to the serious nature of the incident that had prompted the commander of Fort Benson to take personal charge of the rescue operation.

Riding beside him was Lieutenant Hardacre.

The scout wasted no time in lengthy explanations.

141

'You guys have arrived in the nick of time. There ain't a moment to lose. The wagon train is over the far side of the ridge. Let's hope you ain't too late to save them.'

'Looks like you have things sewn up here tight as a banker's fist, Jim,' remarked Sourby. 'Can we leave you to look after these rats?'

'Sure thing, Colonel. The main thing now is saving those immigrants from Yellow Knife's revenge. Although it ain't all his fault.'

Claymaker aimed an accusing finger at the cowering outlaws. 'It was this scum deliberately causing a range fire then killing his son that caused all the ruckus in the first place. Once I tell him that Running Bear really is still alive, I reckon he'll call his braves off.'

Colonel Sourby was not so sure. He gave the scout's support for Yellow Knife a sceptical response. 'We'll see about that, Jim. My first priority is to save those settlers any way I can. If'n he don't surrender. . . .' His hand gripped the sabre more tightly to emphasise his meaning. 'I'll leave a couple of men here to help you corral these critters until its safe to come down to the train.'

'Obliged for that, colonel. These varmints need watching closely and I'm plum tuckered out.' It was then that he realized he had not come out of the fracas unscathed. Blood was seeping through his jacket. Unbuttoning it, he saw that one of the bullets had sliced across his rib cage. Only then did he feel the pain. It was not a serious injury, but would still require bandaging up to staunch the blood.

142

'Private Jackson is our field medic,' Sourby declared. 'He'll soon have you fixed up good as new.'

The colonel saluted with a brisk command to the bugler. 'Sound the charge, corporal. And let's give these redskins a taste of cold steel. That should put the fear of God into them.' Then to the whole troop, he shouted, 'Once we're over the ridge, men, spread out in line for a full blooded charge. You know what to do once we've got them on the run.'

It was clear to the scout that there would be no mercy shown if Yellow Knife decided to put up any serious resistance. Once the cavalry force had left, Claymaker and his two aides hustled the prisoners up on to the ridge to observe the action. The body of Big Bull was slung over a horse. Claymaker had an idea that could prevent the wholesale slaughter that he was certain would follow. Yellow Knife was a proud and resilient warrior chief. He would not back down under any circumstances.

Unless. . . .

By the time they pushed through the surrounding cover of vegetation cloaking the ridge top, the cavalry were lining up in readiness for the charge. The Indians had been taken completely by surprise. With the army on one side and the renewed vigour of the settlers on the other, it was inevitable that much blood would be spilled. And most of it would be of Comanche origin.

There was only one way to bring this slaughter to an end allowing Yellow Knife to save face. Claymaker heaved the dead body of Big Bull into full view. On his head was perched the all-important bearskin head-dress. Sitting behind on the horse so that he could not be seen, it appeared from a distance that Big Bull was still alive.

The scout placed two fingers in his mouth and emitted a piercing screech akin to that of a bald eagle. It was a summons, universal among the tribes, to pay heed for some vital news.

His aim was to alert the chief to the presence of his medicine-man. The ploy was successful. Yellow Knife was poised on the far side of the valley gathering his reserves together when he heard the evocative ulula-tion.

Claymaker raised both arms of the medicine-man towards the Heavens. In a suitably gruff yet sonorous intonation, he called out for all to hear.

'Running Bear lives!! Running Bear lives!!'

The crystal clear announcement took some moments to make its startling presence felt. Once again the haunting declaration echoed across the valley.

'Again, I Big Bull declare that Running Bear lives!! The chief's son is alive!!'

It was all that was needed to bring the threatened onslaught to a stumbling halt. In total disarray, the Indian charge faltered then disintegrated.

Colonel Sourby soon had them on the run in panic-stricken flight. With all the fire knocked out of them, it was a simple matter for the seasoned troopers to encircle the Indians and force them to surrender.

A relieved Jim Claymaker withdrew. He lowered the

body of Big Bull to the ground for later collection. 'OK boys, let's get down there and join in the cele-brations.' That was when he noticed that one of the gang was missing.

'Where's Gemmel?' he blurted out.

'Looks like he's scarpered,' snarled Beedon, 'and left us to take the rap.'

Claymaker cursed his stupidity. He'd been so engrossed in trying to save Yellow Knife's hide that he had overlooked what a slippery snake Ira Gemmel really was. Now the skunk had disappeared.

But the scout had a good idea where the skulking trader would have headed.

THIRTEEN

THE REAPER'S CALL

'Is it all right if'n I leave these critters in your capable hands, fellas?' Claymaker enquired of the two troopers. 'I have me a notion as to what Gemmel has in mind. And he needs to be stopped.'

'What might that be, Jim?' asked Jackson the medic while attempting to bandage up Kramer's wounded shoulder. The other man kept a beady eye on the others.

'If'n he gets rid of Running Bear, the chief's son, there's no witness left that could testify against him. A court of law could not be able to convict him of murder. The rat would be free as a bird.'

'I'd sure be willing to stand up and tell what happened if the court went easy on me,' declared Beedon. 'That skunk has abandoned us without a second's thought. He deserves everything that's coming to him.'

146

'That's all right for you to say now,' Claymaker rasped acidly. 'But it won't stop him killing Running Bear, will it?'

Beedon remained silent. There was no answer to that piece of logic.

'Keep these jaspers under close guard, boys,' Claymaker exhorted the troopers as he leapt on to Big Bull's horse. 'We'll have them for fire-raising if nothing else.'

He was just about to gallop off, but paused. 'And one more favour you could do me.' The troopers listened intently. 'There's a Miss Stapleton down there somewhere. Me and her are . . . kinda walking out.' The army men couldn't suppress knowing looks. 'I'd be obliged if'n you could tell her that I'm OK and will be back soon as I've finished some unfinished business.'

'Be our pleasure, Jim,' Trooper Jackson replied. 'Do you want us to say what it's all about?'

Claymaker shook his head. 'That's for the ears of the wagon master only – an old mountain man called Griff Reed.'

And with that final comment, he rode off.

The conniving trader had an hour's start. Not a lot, but he was mounted on a horse that had been rested and fed. If Claymaker was to overtake him, he would need to take a short cut to the Comanche encampment in the Sangre de Cristos range. And the best way was to backtrack across the Canadian to the Costilla Valley. That was the way Coyote Calhoun had hoped to lead the settlers to Santa Rosa.

The fire would have burned itself out by now. And it would save him a good half day's travel. Much as he would have dearly loved to check if his betrothed was still alive, duty had to come first. Catching up with Gemmel and bringing him to justice was an urgent priority.

If'n the skunk managed to carry out his heinous plan to erase the one person who could give evidence against him, a full blown Indian war would surely follow. And this time Yellow Knife would call on other tribes to help him. Kiowa, Apache and Cheyenne would not hesitate to take up arms against the white invaders. A blood bath of unimaginable consequence would be inevitable.

Ira Gemmel had to be stopped at all costs.

Nevertheless, before leaving on his vital mission, the scout couldn't resist skirting the upper rim above the valley. He drew Blaize to a halt overlooking the body strewn battleground. Most of them were Comanche. The settlers had certainly given a good account of themselves. Carefully he studied the ragged circle of wagons.

A fervent entreaty was despatched upstairs that Lavinia had survived. Was she down there now helping to clear up the chaos instigated by Ira Gemmel? Or was she now occupying one of the plots over to the left marked by wooden crosses?

It was a futile guessing game in which Green River Jim could not become embroiled. All he could do now was remain positive and do his duty. His mouth tightened into a thin line of determination and resolve.

Dragging the appaloosa away from the rim, he set a course towards the north west.

The blackened terrain of the Costilla Valley still smouldered in places. Claymaker kept to the higher ground pushing Big Bull's mustang as hard as he dared. By noon of the second day he was following the rimrock when he spotted a twirl of dust down below. A lone rider was following the twisting network of canyons that took him ever deeper into the mountain fastness.

Although only a distant speck, Claymaker knew that it was a white man from the wide-brimmed dark hat he was wearing. So it had to be Gemmel. The plateauland across which he himself was travelling encompassed much rougher terrain. But sticking to the more direct high level route, and barring any accidents, he should reach the Indian camp before his quarry.

And so it proved. Though how much time he had gained was anybody's guess. He needed to make his presence felt. And quickly.

He halted on the edge of the camp and removed a white piece of cloth from his saddle bag and tied it to the barrel of his rifle. He had obtained it from the medical pack of Trooper Jackson with just this need in mind. Riding in without due warning was a sure way to get chopped down by a flurry of arrows. The flag of peace was held aloft for all to see.

Then, in a loud stentorian voice imbuing all the commanding urgency he could muster, the scout announced his arrival.

'Pay heed to my words, people of the Comanche nation. I, Black Hair, have returned to your homeland in peace. This time I bring good wishes from your revered Chief Yellow Knife who was overjoyed to learn that his son is alive. He has given his approval and authority for me to come here to protect Running Bear.'

He paused to allow the full import of his declaration to take effect.

Within minutes, the tepees had emptied. A host of Indians appeared. What he had to say next would determine his fate. He needed to get it just right. After all, the last time he had been here was as a prisoner staked out awaiting a painful termination. These people would harbour deep suspicions regarding his entreaty.

Gingerly he nudged the mustang into the camp. Any second he expected an arrow to zing his way. But the flag of truce and his claim to have the endorsement of their chief had clearly made an impact. Outright hostility slowly changed to curiosity.

'Yellow Knife has sent me to challenge a bad man who is coming to finish the job he started when thinking he had killed Running Bear. That man is one you have trusted to supply weapons and firewater in exchange for hides and gold. But he speaks with a forked tongue. He is the trader from Santa Rosa called Ira Gemmel.'

This allegation certainly had them muttering amongst themselves.

'I, Black Hair, am a true friend to the Comanche.

150

You know that I have always spoken the truth and treated the Comanche with respect and fairness. Gemmel blamed me for a crime that he and his men had committed. Will you now support me in caring for Running Bear against the two-faced traitor until your chief returns?'

That was when one of the elders stepped forward. There was a grim look pasted across his wizened features. He pointed an accusing finger. 'Why does Black Hair ride the horse belonging to Big Bull our medicine-man?'

Nods of anger greeted this allegation. Hands tightened on tomahawks and lances as they advanced towards him.

'Gemmel killed your shamen when he tried to tell Yellow Knife the good news.' Once again his own survival hung by a thread. He stifled the tremor of fear that might cause his voice to waver. 'This is another reason why I have come here today. To avenge the great name of Big Bull. But there is no time to lose. The evil one will be here soon. We must prepare a suitable reception for him so that Running Bear's life is protected.'

The threat of Gemmel's imminent arrival seemed to galvanize them into action. The scout was waved forward. Tense muscles relaxed. His breathing settled to a more steady rhythm. It had been a close call. But the business of thwarting Gemmel's bid to escape his just desserts still remained.

How would one man alone be able to finish the job he had started in the midst of all these people?

Then it struck him. The answer was as clear as a church bell. If'n he hadn't arrived early they would have had no reason to doubt Gemmel's sincerity. All it would have taken was some poison slipped into a drink and administered to Running Bear. Easily achieved. Then he could leave before the lethal concoction did its work.

'Black Hair lies!' The sonorous accusation rang out across the encampment. The rat had arrived sooner than expected. 'It is he who is the true killer. This traitor rides the horse of Big Bull because it is he who pulled the trigger. Now he seeks to finish the task. I will avenge you by putting a bullet into the two-faced dog.'

Once again condemnatory eyes fastened on to the army scout. The advantage had suddenly shifted full circle. Gemmel's rifle lifted. The lever snapped down pushing a deadly load into the breech. A finger tightening on the trigger. The smile of satisfaction filled the scout with loathing mixed with frustration.

Nobody moved. Ambiguous glances flitted between the two adversaries. Who was spitting venom?

Claymaker was stymied. He didn't want to die. Nor did he want this odious specimen to hoodwink these simple people. But what could he do?

Just when he figured the bell was about to toll, the unexpected occurred.

FOURTEEN

MIXED BLESSINGS

Gemmel threw up his arms and pitched forward. An arrow was sticking out of his leg. 'Aaaaaaagh!' he screamed. Falling to the ground, he clutched at the injury.

That was when Yellow Knife emerged from the cover of a clump of pine trees. He was accompanied by those warriors who had survived the battle. It had clearly not been meant as a killing loose.

'Stay where you are, Black Hair,' declared the chief. His command was supported by the raised weapons of his braves. 'Your trickery of speaking through the mouth of Big Bull persuaded me to surrender when the blue coats arrived. It is lucky that such a commander as Colonel Sourby was in charge. He is a fair and just leader. He accepted my word that no further attacks would happen if he allowed us to return home to the Sangre de Cristos.'

The chief led his men down into the camp and stopped directly facing the scout.

Claymaker raised the white flag. 'Yellow Knife sees that I have come in peace. If Black Hair was a snake in the grass, would he dare to return here?'

The chief held the scout's unflinching gaze before nodding slowly. 'I smoked pipe of peace with white chief,' he continued. 'He told me it was this snake who shot and killed Big Bull. It was as you say. He was shot to stop me learning that the Great Spirit had saved my son.' Staring eyes fixed the cringing backstabber with a malignant glare. 'For that Gemmel will die a slow death.'

Yellow Knife signalled for two braves to grab the cowering brigand.

'As for my son,' he said turning to address Claymaker. 'I want to believe that what you told me near wagons before battle was truth. But you have tried to deceive my people with your claims that I, Yellow Knife sent you here. What have you to say? Your next words will determine if you live or die alongside this piece of dung.'

Claymaker hung his head. 'It is true, great chief. But only to prove that I played no part in the crime against your son. I came here to stop Gemmel completing his evil work. Have I not helped you in the past when times were hard? Black Hair is a man to be trusted.'

Yellow Knife held up a hand to stem the flow. 'You have said enough. Black Hair has indeed proved to be a true friend of the Comanche. But first I wish to hear the truth from the lips of Running Bear himself.'

Both white men were disarmed and held firmly in the grip of braves allotted to stand guard over them. The chief was taking no chances of betrayal. He strode purposefully towards his tepee and entered alongside his squaw Swooping Owl. They remained inside for a good ten minutes.

The sky darkened overhead as storm clouds threatened to unleash their fury. Claymaker shivered. Was it a sign of impending doom? An owl hooted lending its eerie refrain to the nail-biting atmosphere.

No words were spoken by either of the prisoners. Each was cocooned in his own macabre thoughts. How the next few moments would play out was now in the lap of the Great Manitou.

Finally the chief emerged along with his retinue who lined up behind. Blank faces gave nothing away. Yellow Knife looked from one to the other. A grave scowl imbuing deep-seated hatred spread across the leathery features as he jabbed a accusing finger at the slobbering trader.

'Take this poisonous cur and stake him out. He will suffer a thousand agonies for what he has done. Death will come as a blessed relief.'

Claymaker released the pent-up tension gripping his whole frame. But he had other plans in mind for the double-dealing varmint.

'This man deserves all you promise, great chief. But would it not be better for him to answer for his crimes in the white man's court? I, Black Hair will ensure that justice prevails. I will also arrange a peace

155

treaty between our peoples that guarantees Comanche land holdings in exchange for permission that other settlers can cross to start a new life in the West.'

Claymaker was sincere in his protestation although there was no guarantee that any such undertaking would be held binding in the future. Many treaties had been made in the past. Few had succeeded.

But warming to his cause, he pressed on. 'The Comanche will continue to receive supplies in times of hardship as part of the agreement.' Then a note of caution crept into the address. 'But take law into your own hands and the Great White Father in Washington will be displeased. Blue coats will flood the land forcing your people on to reservations. Does Yellow Knife want that?'

The chief balked at the threat. But he was a realist and knew the way the wind was blowing. 'It is as you say,' he concurred somewhat disconsolately. 'Take this swine and do with him as you will.'

The journey back to the wagon train was accomplished without incident. Gemmel's injury had been dressed and he was feeling much relieved at having escaped Comanche justice. With the threat of a painful end lifted, his thoughts reverted to the devious chicanery for which he excelled. Numerous bribes were offered en route to strike a deal. When these failed to work, toothless threats followed. All were like water off a duck's back to the loyal army scout.

Once they rejoined the settlers, Claymaker handed the killer over to the tender mercies of Colonel Sourby and his men.

Many of the immigrants who had lost money recognized the double-dealing fraudster. They were all for administering instant justice to the man who had caused all their misery and distress. With over a dozen of their men folk occupying makeshift graves, there was little stomach for an official trial that might result in the snake wriggling free.

It was only the fervent exhortations of Colonel Sourby supported by his army scout that persuaded them otherwise. Their combined emphasis that adhering to the law of the land was the only way to bring civilized behaviour to the wild frontier of the American West finally brought order to what could have become an ugly situation.

Griff Reed then encouraged the settlers to ready themselves to continue the trek to Santa Rosa. 'We still have a good two week's travel ahead of us, folks,' he stressed. 'Let's hope that Yellow Knife is more amenable now.'

'Reckon I persuaded him that co-operation will be far more profitable for his people than confrontation,' Claymaker added, with the further boost, 'You won't get any trouble now that Broken Lance is out of the picture.'

Once he learned that Lavinia Stapleton had been a tower of strength to the settlers in their greatest hour of need, Claymaker was now eager to seek her out. With Ira Gemmel and his men securely tethered and in the firm grip of the cavalry, he moved off on what he hoped would be a most gratifying quest.

He was pulled up short by a startled exclamation from Fletcher Mason. 'Well I'll be darned,' he blurted out. 'If'n it ain't Bart Travis!'

The lawyer had just arrived back from a supply expedition he had accompanied to the nearest trading post at Brogden's Reach. His earnest claim was aimed at none other than Ira Gemmel. Not haling from Concordia, the lawyer had never seen the braggart in the flesh before.

He was peering hard at a well-thumbed photograph in his hand.

Claymaker turned back at this astonishing revelation. 'So this rat has changed his name, eh? I can understand why, now that I've learned the truth about him.' His next remark was aimed at Mason. 'So you must be a lawman come after him for breaking jail. But I figure this territory has a bigger claim on the skunk. Guess you'll have to wait in line, Mason.'

The man he knew only as Ira Gemmel was struck dumb, astounded by this sudden exposure of his past misdeeds.

'No, Mister Claymaker, I'm just a regular lawyer.' Mason went on to reveal the true nature of his journey west in search of the illusive Bart Travis.

'I'm well aware of this guy's dubious dealings in Concordia and that he broke jail. But that's not why I'm after him.' He paused to focus his attention on the dumb-founded Travis. 'This man who now calls himself Ira Gemmel has been left a sizeable legacy by

158

a rich uncle. He probably never knew Ezekial J. Travis, the celebrated cotton merchant from West Virginia. My company was employed to track Bart Travis down as being the sole surviving relative of the late entrepreneur.'

'So all the time he was trying to cheat people, he could have be living the high life.' Claymaker made no effort to contain an outburst of laughter. Tears of mirth ran down his face. Tears of pure anguish were reserved for Bart Travis. For him the future was bleak. 'All he can look forward to now is a lengthy prison sentence, or more likely a hangman's noose.'

Still chuckling uproariously, the scout stumbled away. All he wanted was to see Lavinia. But would she still feel the same about him? His nerves were in a tangled mess. Nonetheless, he couldn't suppress another bout of hilarity regarding the satisfactory outcome of the Gemmel-Travis fiasco.

Then all of sudden there she was – the woman of his dreams. Lavinia was returning from having completed her ablutions down on the river bank. As she drew close, his heart began beating like a steam hammer.

'What's amusing you then, Jim Claymaker,' the comely female admonished him. 'Do I look that unsightly?'

'No, no,' he hurriedly assured her. 'It ain't you. I'll tell you about it later. All I want to know is. . . .' His hastily prepared speech stumbled to an undignified halt. 'Well, what I meant to say was . . . Would you . . . Do you figure we might . . . When all this business is

159

over, will you. . . ?'

'The answer to what you're trying to say is. . . . Yes!'

A grin wider than the Mississippi spread across the scout's dirt-smeared countenance. 'Then I hope you like oranges,' was all he could blurt out.